ELLEN ELIZABETH HUNTER

Ellen Eliz Hunter

MURDER AT THE HOLIDAY FLOTILLA

Magnolia Mysteries

www.magnoliamysteries.com

Published by:
Magnolia Mysteries

This is a work of fiction.

ISBN 978-0-9755404-8-0

Cover and book design by Tim Doby
Photo Credit: John Domoney, ©2003
j domoney imaging, inc., www.jdomoneyimaging.com

Also by Ellen Elizabeth Hunter

Murder on the Ghost Walk

Murder on the Candlelight Tour

Murder at the Azalea Festival

Murder at Wrightsville Beach

Murder on the ICW

Murder on the Cape Fear

Christmas Wedding

Murder at the Bellamy Mansion

Murder at the Holiday Flotilla

Visit Ellen's website,
www.ellenhunter.com

In memory of:
Dolly
Beloved Pet
1995 – 2010

Notes

This book was inspired by the Last Will & Testament of my g5 grandmother, Reuhama Wood, who died in 1825 at the age of ninety. In the will she bequeathed "the residue of my New Orleans legacy" to her daughter. But what was the legacy? No one in the family knows.

Taking that curious tidbit of information, and setting the story in Wilmington and Brunswick County, I have researched the Colonial period there to construct a plot that leads my heroines on a search for their own legacy.

But what name should I assign to Ashley and Melanie's fictitious ancestors? That would require some care. For just about any English surname I might think of, there would be a family currently alive with that name – and might they object? What to do? I decided I would use the surnames of various lines of my own family: Wood, Humphreys, Hughes, Jordan, and Craighead.

A great big thank you to the following folks: Faye Brock for her expertise in real estate matters; Dave Anderson for his creative suggestions; Linda Linares, Linda Price, Katie Brinkley, Joyce Zimmerman, Kay and "Shack" Shackelford for cameo roles.

Thanks also to Scott Randolph of Bill Black Cadillac for allowing me to explore the interior of the Cadillac Escalade and for details about the security features of the Cadillac DTS.

As usual my hat is off to my fabulous designer, Tim Doby.

My study of our Colonial history was made real by my genealogical research of my patriot ancestors. They are:

William Hunter 1750-1837
Sergeant, 4th PA Continental Regiment 1777-1780
Sergeant, Commander-in-Chief's Guard 1780-1783
Guarded General Washington at the Battle of Connecticut
Farms; Battle at King's Bridge NY; Battle of Yorktown VA.

Lewis Humphreys 1753-1805
Private, 1st Delaware Continental Regiment 1776
Seaman Maryland Ship *Defence* 1777

Captain Jonathan Wood 1740-1803
Master of Vessels 1762-1774
Philadelphia

Felix Hughes 1723-1805
Signed petition to Congress from inhabitants of
Laurel Hill 1783

A special thank you to my friends at
The Colonel Arthur Lee Forbis Chapter
National Society Daughters of the American Revolution
for sustaining my patriotism.

1

"My stars, we'll be eating turkey leftovers for days," Aunt Ruby said. "There's enough food in that kitchen to feed an army."

"Amen to that," her husband Binkie said with a satisfied grin, looking like he might just rub his tummy. "You know, there's an ingredient in turkey that aids with sleep."

"These little guys didn't have any turkey, and just look at them snoring away," my brother-in-law Cam said with the proud smile of a doting uncle.

After a bountiful Thanksgiving dinner we were gathered in my library for coffee, eggnog, brandy, and dessert. The beautiful red room, once the epitome of a refined Victorian library, has been transformed into a first floor nursery: folded baby clothes stacked in side chairs, a downstairs changing table, and two baby carriers. Packages of Pampers filled the cherrywood book shelf where once a collection of leatherbound nineteenth century classics resided.

The baby carriers cradled my precious babies, identical twin boys born in September. My sister Melanie could not tell them apart so after asking their daddy Jon to identify them, she had affixed yellow post-its to the hoods of the carriers. One post-it read Peter, the other read Jonathan.

"Very funny," I told her.

Jon and I had named our sons for our fathers: Peter Wilkes for me, Jonathan Campbell for Jon.

Melanie snickered and settled on the big red leather sofa, snuggling into the crook of the arm of her hopelessly smitten husband Cam. "Now, honestly, Ashley, tell me the truth. Don't fib now. Can you really tell them apart?"

I lifted a cup of foamy eggnog to my lips. From my lips to my hips, I reminded myself. But that didn't stop me. Carrying those babies had sure caused me to gain a lot of weight. Still, it wasn't the babies who were now pouring a thousand calories worth of eggnog down my throat. I had only myself to blame for my lack of will power. In fact my precious babies were sleeping angelically, the picture of innocence.

"Yes, I can tell them apart. What kind of a mother would I be if I didn't know my own babies?"

Melanie eyed me knowingly. "I can always tell when she's fibbing," she told the others.

"Well, I can usually tell them apart," I confessed. "Definitely when they're naked."

"I can tell them apart even when they're dressed," Jon informed us. "Even now with the little cherubs asleep. Jonathan's eyebrows are set a little higher on his forehead than Peter's."

"They are?" I questioned, leaning forward to stare intently at my infant sons, comparing their tiny faces, one with the other. Sure enough, Jon was right. I took his hand. "You are so smart."

He beamed at me. Jon loves it when I praise him.

"Perfect ending to a perfect day," Binkie said with a contented groan of pleasure. "But nothing can top seeing Scarlett in the Macy's parade."

The day *had* been perfect. A perfect Thanksgiving for the Wilkes sisters and their family. I am Ashley Wilkes, historic preservationist and old-house restorer, in business with my husband, architect Jon Campbell.

My sister Melanie is Wilmington's star realtor and, in January, will assume the office of President of the North Carolina Association of Realtors.

Aunt Ruby and Uncle Binkie were here of course, having spent the day with us. They are the only family we have left and thankfully live just a short walk away on Front and Ann streets, while Jon and I live on Nun Street between Second and Third in Wilmington's downtown historic district. Nun Street is named for the nuns would cared for the Civil War wounded, turning the Benjamin Beery mansion into a hospital. Now the proud residence is a popular Bed & Breakfast, called The Verandas after its many porches.

Melanie and I also have a half sister, Scarlett, who lives up North. She is just the sweetest thing, and so down to earth, you'd never guess she is one of Broadway's brightest musical stars. She lives in New York City with her stock broker husband, Ray.

Scarlett has the lead female role in the revival of *Guys and Dolls* on Broadway. And this morning she had performed in front of Macy's and been on national television. Playing the role of Miss Adelaide, Scarlett and the Hot Box Girls put on a big production number "A Bushel and a Peck" from the show.

"What a thrill it was to see Scarlett," I said. "I can't wait till she and Ray get here to share the holidays with us."

Scarlett and Ray are committed to demanding careers, and for that reason were unable to fly south to Wilmington for the Thanksgiving holidays. And then we found out that Scarlett would be in the big Macy's Thanksgiving Day parade. What an honor! But they gave us their word they would be with us for Christmas. They own a getaway at Wrightsville Beach, an ocean-front cottage named *Bella Aqua*. Aunt Ruby told them, "You'd better come to us or you will have the North Carolina contingent camped on the doorstep of your Manhattan townhouse: howling babies, diaper bags and all."

"When are you putting up your tree?" my brother-in-law Cam asked.

"I don't think we'll have one this year," I replied. "I'm worn out. The thought of all the work it takes to decorate a tree, well, just the thought exhausts me." I yawned, which I do frequently these days. "And it's not like the little guys will notice."

Cam squeezed Melanie's shoulder. "Melanie's got Linda Price decorating for us, starting tomorrow. Now tomorrow night we're meeting you at Airlie for the light show. And then on Saturday night, y'all are coming out to the lodge for the flotilla party. Right?"

I stifled a chuckle. It always tickles me to hear my California brother-in-law say "y'all" just like the downhome family he'd married into.

"Ashley and I have to work tomorrow," Jon said.

"We're babysitting." Binkie was delighted.

Jon went on, "But we never miss the Airlie lights or the flotilla. Although we may have to hire a truck to haul the baby equipment out to the Waterway."

"I was thinking," Melanie said. "Why don't I buy some baby furniture and supplies and keep them at our house? Then you won't have to drag everything along with you. I've got eight bedrooms; surely I can devote one of them to my nephews."

"Oh, sis, you've given us so much already."

"But I want to. No arguments. It's settled then. We'll set up one of the smaller bedrooms as a baby guest room." She smiled, very pleased with herself.

I helped myself to one of the several desserts we had carried into the library and arranged on the coffee table. "Cam, these chocolate pecan tarts are to die for." Cameron Jordan, a high-powered, successful television producer, is an amateur pastry chef, insisting that rolling out pastry dough is a form of relaxation for him. What a treat for all of us.

"I'm so stuffed, I'm about to nod off like your babies," Cam said with a contented sigh.

"What about your fruit cake, Aunt Ruby?" Jon asked. "Talk about delicious! And that cornbread stuffing you made to go with the turkey. Please be sure to leave me some for tomorrow. I'm like Binkie, there's nothing better than Thanksgiving leftovers."

Jon and Cam had set up a grill in the garden early that morning and smoked a plump turkey breast. Then, with everyone bringing their favorite dishes, we had ourselves a feast.

"I don't know if I can move," Melanie sighed, "but I've got something to show you." Groaning dramatically, she struggled to her feet and went over to the desk to lift a large flat box she had brought in and placed there before dinner. She carried it over to the coffee table. "Give me a hand here, Cam sweetheart. Just move those plates over to the side table."

Cam and Binkie hurried to clear the coffee table for Melanie's box.

"Another present for the babies?" I asked my sister. "Mel, you've given them so much. You are just too generous."

Melanie shook her long auburn hair. "No, that's not it. This is something else. I don't know what to make of all this." She set the box down – it didn't appear to be heavy – straightened up and folded her arms across her chest.

"Remember when we sold Mama's house?" she asked.

"Of course, I remember," I replied. How do you forget something as monumental as parting with your family home-place? Our sweet mama had died two and a half years ago. Daddy had gone on to heaven several years before her, and I'm sure had been there to greet her with a kiss and an embrace when she arrived, although they both had been too young to leave us when they did.

"Remember all the stuff from the attic that we stored in that rental storage unit?" Melanie asked.

"Naturally, I remember. There was so much and we did-n't know what to do with it all. We were overwhelmed." A rented storage unit had been the ideal solution for the boxes and trunks we didn't have the time or the heart to go through, and for the odd pieces of furniture we didn't have a home for. The nice furniture, Melanie and I had divided. And things that didn't fit into our homes went to Joyce Zimmerman's "Just Like New" consignment shop on Kerr Avenue.

Melanie went on. "Then, when you and Jon restored the hunting lodge for Cam and me, we had tons of space. So I had all the stuff moved from the storage unit to my house."

"I didn't know that."

"Guess I forgot to tell you, little sis.

"Anyway, things were a bit slow at the office this week, what with the holiday and this dreadful housing market, so Aunt Ruby and Binkie came out on Tuesday and together we went through some of the boxes. What a hodgepodge. Valuables mixed in with trifles. So much stuff we still don't know what to do with it all."

"Our little bungalow on Front Street is bursting at the seams," Aunt Ruby said. "This is not a decision for Binkie and me. You girls have got to decide what gets saved, what goes to Goodwill, and what gets . . . well, tossed. But you know we'll help."

I stared at Melanie. "But what's in the box? You must have found something worth saving for you to tote it along today."

"You're right. You have to take a look at this. Binkie says they are important." And with that, she lifted the lid off the box.

I leaned forward to peer inside. "Old papers? You want me to go through old papers? On Thanksgiving?"

Binkie, who has been like a father to me since Daddy

passed, told me kindly, "Not just any old papers, Ashley dear. You don't understand. These are more than trivial papers. They are important, historical family documents."

I reached into the box and lifted out a sheaf of folded papers.

"Careful," Binkie cautioned.

Gingerly, I unfolded a document that was three pages in length. Each page measured at least twenty by fourteen inches in size. And every inch of the paper was covered with elaborate hand-written script. And tiny ink blotches. I stared at the sentences, my eyes fairly popping wide. The documents were original, not photocopies.

"This looks like a late-eighteenth, early-nineteenth century document." I'd had an introduction to historic documents in one of my graduate classes at the Savannah College of Arts and Design.

"Are you saying you can read that gobbledygook?" Melanie asked. "It's English, I can see that, but who can make sense of it?"

"Why, I can," Binkie said. "But I've only had time for a cursory perusal. Just a quick glance to see what we are dealing with."

"I feel sure I can too," I said. "Just takes a bit of getting used to."

I carefully turned to the last page and discovered what I had expected to find: a list of witnesses' signatures.

"This is a last will and testament. And these names are the signatures of the witnesses," I said as I scanned the document for a date. "Oh, here it is. Here's the date the will was written and witnessed. April 2, 1805."

I turned to the last page. "And this is when the will was proved, April 30, 1805."

"Proved? What does that mean?" Cam asked, leaning forward on the sofa to gaze down at the sheaf of papers I'd spread on the coffee table.

"Similar to probate. This means the person who wrote this will died sometime between April 2nd and April 30th in 1805."

As a history professor, Binkie would recognize the significance of these early documents. "Have you read these papers?" I asked him. There were other folded documents in the box as well as the will.

"Just a brief look. Long enough to know they are of value. Wills and property appraisals. Either the originals or handwritten copies. There are bonds of marriage as well, and marriage registrations."

Turning to the others, he explained, "In the Colonial era they had what was called 'a bond of marriage.' The man had to pledge a sum of money to a magistrate. If he did not go through with the marriage, he forfeited the bond to his fiancée."

Melanie pursed her lips. "Not a bad custom." She squeezed back onto the sofa between Cam and Binkie.

"I'd have put up a bond for you," Cam said, teasing. "A big bond." Or perhaps he was not teasing.

Binkie rose and came around the coffee table to sit by my side and give me a reassuring hug. "It's a treasure trove, Ashley dear. Here is proof of your ancestors. Some of these papers predate the Revolutionary War."

"We still have boxes and boxes to explore," Melanie said. "These papers were in an old trunk."

"Would someone turn the lamp a little brighter," I asked as I peered intently at the papers spread before me. "The cover sheet reads, 'Samuel Wood's Will, proven April 30, 1805.' Aunt Ruby, have you ever heard of Samuel Wood? Who was he?"

Aunt Ruby replied thoughtfully, "Your mother was a Chastain, as I am, of course. Of the Savannah Chastains. And Scarlett is of the Chastain line. Your father was a Wilkes, to state the obvious. His mother was a Humphreys. And if memory serves me correctly, her grandmother was a Wood. Margaret Wood whose grandfather was a Wood. I do recall that Margaret Wood married a Civil War veteran named John Humphreys. I reckon this Samuel Wood was an ancestor of Margaret Wood."

"I vaguely remember Daddy telling me we had an ancestor who served in the Revolutionary War," Melanie said. "Perhaps this Samuel Wood was that patriot."

I said, "Let me read what I can of this will. The language is very formal so bear with me.

"In the name of God, Amen, I Samuel Wood of the County of Brunswick and state of North Carolina, being weak in body but of sound and disposing mind and memory, blessed be God, do make and publish this my last will and testament in manner as follows. First, I recommend my soul to God, and my body to the Earth and as touching such worldly goods as it hath pleased God to bestow on me in life, I give and dispose of them as follows."

I paused, studying the document. "There's a word here I can't make out. Then he goes on to leave three daughters the sum of five dollars each. But one also receives a horse and saddle."

"Five dollars? He must not have thought much of his daughters," Cam said.

Binkie said, "No doubt he was relying on their husbands to provide for them. And remember, this was 1805. Five dollars was a lot of money in 1805. Continue with your reading, Ashley dear."

I was skimming along. "Let me summarize. You don't want to hear every word. He left his house and his lot to his son, David Wood, and upon David's death the house and lot were to go to David's wife, then oldest child, in that order.

"Then he leaves various small items to several named people."

"Possibly servants?" Melanie asked.

"Ah. Here in item five he mentions the son David again. 'I give and bequeath to my son David and his heirs and assigns all my lands, my longleaf pine forests, my personal estate, cash on hand, money at interest, together with all the residue of my Wilmington treasure.'"

"Wilmington treasure!" Melanie exclaimed. "What is that?"

"Lastly he appoints his wife Elizabeth to serve as his executor."

"And the will was proven, you say," Jon asked.

I pushed the sheaf of papers toward him, and pointed to the cover sheet. "See. Right there it says, Samuel Wood's will.

Proven April 30, 1805, and recorded in the surrogate's office at Smithville in . . . something . . . looks like l-i-b-r . . ."

"Library?" Aunt Ruby suggested.

"Perhaps. To continue, in l-i-b-r at folio folio - folio is repeated twice - so, folio 18, and then there's another word I can't make out."

"May I have a look, Ashley?"

As I passed the will to Binkie, I told Cam, "In case you don't know, Southport was originally known as Smithville."

"I think I heard that," Cam responded.

Binkie slipped on readers. "Ah, yes, the word appears to be 'of wills.' But the two words are joined together. And then there is a signature. Jacob somebody. Can't make out the last name. But there is a capital S following the surname with some swirls so perhaps he was the Surrogate."

"But what do you make of the treasure?" Melanie asked.

"Never heard anything about a treasure," I said, "but I've heard about the old Wood estate in Brunswick County for most of my life. Haven't you, Binkie?"

"Most definitely," he replied. "One of the area's oldest families. And to think they may be your ancestors."

I continued, "And here is the oddest thing, the boys' pediatrician is Amy Wood who inherited the Wood estate. That is where Jon and I are going tomorrow. Talk about coincidences. She asked us to look at the house because she'd like to restore it. And now, to think we might be related. Seems uncanny."

No one remarked. We exchanged quizzical looks with each other. Then Cam broke the silence. "Has it occurred to anyone but me that if there is a family fortune floating around Brunswick County somewhere, our lovely brides here could very well be the heirs to a Colonial-era treasure."

2

The next morning, after showing Aunt Ruby and Binkie our babies' paraphernalia and explaining the function of each item, Aunt Ruby exclaimed, "My stars, times have surely changed."

Jon said, "We can't thank you enough. We know the little guys will be safe with you two in charge. And you've got our cell number. Call if you have any question, no matter how trivial."

"You go on to your job and don't worry about a thing," Binkie reassured us. "Ruby and I will have the time of our lives, playing with these precious babies."

"They're angels when they're sleeping," I said. "Don't let them give you a hard time when they awake."

"We won't," Ruby said. "You go on now and don't keep your client waiting."

"We're quite excited," Jon said. "This just might be the oldest house we've ever tackled."

"I've always wanted to see that house," I said.

With promises to check on them often, Jon and I kissed our babies goodbye, then drove across Memorial Bridge to Brunswick County. We crossed Eagle Island where the Battleship North Carolina is dry-docked, and picked up River Road at Belville.

"The discovery of that old will has caused me to think about the colonial period. History was made here along River Road," I said to Jon. "Look, there's the plaque for Alfred Moore." Moore had been a captain in the First North Carolina Continental Regiment. His grandfather had been Colonel Maurice Moore, one of the founders of Brunswick Town in 1720. Alfred Moore had been a defender of Brunswick Town when the British attacked and razed the small village in 1776.

The further south we drove, the denser the forests grew. Pine forests and more pine forests.

Eventually we veered left onto Plantation Road and drove by the entrance to Orton Plantation. After 126 years in the Sprunt family, Orton had a new owner. "I can't get over that the buyer is a direct descendant of Roger Moore," I told Jon. "How cool is that? Wonder how he'll restore the property."

Jon glanced over at me. "I've heard he has a good track record and I'd love for us to get in on that project, wouldn't you?"

"An opportunity to work on Orton would be a dream come true and so good for our careers."

"The Coastal Land Trust holds conservation easements

that cover most of the Orton property, so I don't expect much to change. Only improve. Hopefully."

We drove by the entrance to Old Brunswicktown, a wrought iron gate set in a white stucco wall, two massive stone eagles capping the gate posts.

We were nearing Historic Brunswick Town, now operated by the state. This quiet, picturesque site on the banks of the Cape Fear River has an amazing past. In 1726 Maurice Moore, the son of a former South Carolina governor, founded the port town. Although a small village, Brunswick prospered as a thriving political center because it was the home of two royal governors.

Then came the Stamp Act rebellion, followed by the War of Independence. With the growth of nearby Wilmington and the relocation of the royal governor to New Bern in 1770, few people remained in Brunswick in the spring of 1776 when British redcoats raided and burned the town. For almost two centuries the crumbling remains of the small village lay in obscurity, overgrown with thick foliage. Lost to memory.

Miraculously, in the late 1950s and early 1960s, archaeologists developed an interest in the old settlement and unearthed foundations from Brunswick's original days. The most impressive structure is St. Philip's Anglican Church, four roofless brick walls that date back to 1754.

"Perhaps we'll have time to make a quick detour to St. Philip's before we return home. I love those ancient ruins, those huge arched open windows. The place feels . . . sacred."

Jon reached for my hand. "Yes, it feels that way to me too.

We'll call home and if our boys are not giving Ruby and Binkie a fit, we'll stop for a few minutes.

"You know, Ashley, lately my mind seems to be leaping forward. I find myself daydreaming about the outings we'll take as a family. The interesting places we can show our boys. We have so much to teach them."

"Jon, I've been thinking the same thing. I can't wait. And I'm hoping that we can learn more about my ancestors so we can tell them exactly where they came from. Their legacy."

"Speaking of legacy . . . oh, we've arrived. This is our turn off." Jon steered the Escalade into a narrow country lane. We traveled through a forest of longleaf pines. We found ourselves in a thickly wooded area, nothing out here but trees and more trees, swamps and alligators. After about a mile, we spotted an old house set directly at the end of the driveway.

The house had once been white but with age and disuse had turned a dingy gray. The center section was topped with the traditional Greek Revival pediment. A porch with columns spread across the front. Better days for this house had been a long, long time ago.

Our walk to the front porch was cushioned by pine needles. "Don't see a doorbell," I said.

Jon knocked on the screen door. Dr. Wood did not respond. "She is expecting us."

The heavily wooded property was still and quiet with only the wind sighing in the tops of the tall pines. Then, suddenly, came the noise of incessant howling.

Jon stepped off the porch and looked around. "What in the world is that? Sounds like a pack of wild animals."

"It's coming from the back." The noise grew louder, a baying and a howling. Then furious barking. "Dogs," I said. "It's dogs. But where are they?"

We walked along the side of the house, following the noise of the howling dogs. I couldn't see them but I could hear them.

The ground we hurried over was sandy and littered with pine needles and pine cones. We rounded some oleander bushes and I caught sight of Amy Wood. She was standing near a chain link fence, giant wire clippers in her right hand.

"Amy?" I called.

She turned, saw us, then lifted a palm in warning – back off, back off.

"What?" I wondered out loud.

Quickly, Amy stooped, lowering the wire cutters into position at the bottom of the fence. And began to snip. I could hear the snap, snap of the wire cutters cutting through the heavy wire mesh as she worked to make a small hole.

Once that was done she moved on about three feet, stooped, and cut a second hole. And then another, and another. All the while the dogs grew nearer.

She rose swiftly and ran to our side.

"What are . . .?"

"Shush," she silenced me. "Be quiet."

We stood waiting and watching. For what I couldn't imagine. The barking of the dogs grew incessant and frantic from the other side of the fence.

Then suddenly a small animal popped through one of Amy's holes. A red furry animal about the size of a house cat. Catching sight of us, it ran furiously in the opposite direction, away from us, toward the rear of Amy's property until it vanished into the thick bushes. The animal disappeared in the underbrush.

Just as I was about to turn to Amy to ask her to explain what I was seeing, another red furry animal broke through the fence. Pointy little snoot, red bushy tail. A fox. I was looking at a fox. How small they were. I'd never seen one up close before. And this one broke away, running furiously as it followed the scent of the first fox.

Suddenly, a gray fox pushed through the fence opening as a pack of foxhounds missed it by inches. They howled, and scrambled, trying to break through the fence. Some leapt against the fence, attempting to scale it. Others began pawing the dirt, trying to dig under it. Another tried to squeeze through the hole in the fence only to get caught and with great effort managed to wiggle back to the interior.

In a violent outburst, Amy threw the wire cutters on the ground. "Damn him!" she cried. "Damn him to hell!"

Jon and I looked at each other helplessly. What had we stumbled into? The Amy Wood I knew was a gentle, loving caretaker of babies. My boys took to her right away. Now I was seeing another side of the pediatrician.

Just then a grimy black pickup truck came roaring up the lane, flying, a cloud of dense dust spreading in its wake. The driver braked with a screech mere inches from the rear of our Escalade. Jon dashed toward the man who jumped out of the cab, the door left hanging open, the engine running.

"You almost hit my car," Jon shouted.

The man strode by Jon, as if he wasn't there. He broke into a trot and didn't stop until he was face to face with Dr.

Wood. "You bitch! You did it again. I called the sheriff. Destruction of private property, that's what this is. We'll take you back to court. This time they'll lock you up."

He flung out a hand as if to shove her

"Stop that!" Jon cried. "Don't you dare lay a hand on her." He ran toward her, to defend her.

I was speechless. What in the world was going on?

But Amy was too quick for the thick, balding man. She reached down, grabbed up the wire cutters, and with a quick thrust jabbed the blunt tip into the man's chest. He backed off, yelling, "Now I'll bring charges for assault!"

"You're on my property," Amy cried. She drove the wire cutters further into his chest forcing him to back up. "You're trespassing. Ashley! Call 911. I've got a restraining order against this killer."

She kept pushing the man with the clippers. "Git, you spineless worm. I'll see you in hell. And your spineless boss too."

"You're out of control, woman," the man shouted, but was frantically backing away and backing down from the quarrel.

"You think I'm going to stand by and permit your dogs to rip those helpless creatures to shreds. No way! You tell that scoundrel you work for I won't rest until I see him in jail. Or dead. Whichever comes first. And I hope it's death.

"Now git off my land!" She was holding the wire cutters by their long handles now, swinging them like a baseball bat, aiming for the man's bullet-shaped head.

He turned and ran. As he swung up into his truck, he

looked back and called, "You're crazy, you bitch! You know that. You'll see. You're the one going to jail."

Watching the truck drive down the lane, Amy Wood seemed to be in another world. Vaguely, she turned to us, sighed deeply, and started toward the house. "Come on inside. I'll pour us some iced tea, calm down, and try to explain what's been going on."

We stepped onto a screened porch and followed her into the old-fashioned kitchen. At a quick glance, the kitchen had not been updated since the Fifties. But I had lost interest in appraising the house. "Who was that wild man?" I asked.

"That's Dewey Carter. He manages the place."

"And what did he mean by he'd take you back to court? Has he taken you to court over this feud?"

Amy was sullen. "Yes, but the judge threw it out. The county wants to keep a low-profile on this penned fox hunt controversy."

"But why are the foxes penned?" I asked.

Apparently Jon knew more about the subject than I. "Are they running a penned fox hunt over there?" he asked, anger making his face flush red.

Amy leaned into the refrigerator, withdrew a pitcher of iced tea, then turned and moved toward the kitchen counter. "That's exactly what they're doing."

"What's a penned fox hunt?" I asked.

Amy reached up into the cupboard for three glasses, set them on the counter, and concentrated on pouring tea. Suddenly she stopped what she was doing and pressed her hand over her heart. "I've got to sit down."

I was nearest to her. I took her by the arm and led her over to the kitchen table. "Sit here, Dr. Wood. And let's get you a glass of water, not tea. You don't need caffeine if your heart is racing. Jon, fill a glass with water for her.

"Dr. Wood, are you all right?"

She looked up at me as if truly seeing me for the first time since we arrived. "Yes. I'm OK. They just make me so mad. What they are doing is cruel and inhumane, barbaric, and all for a few measly dollars."

I dropped down into the chair next to her. "Would one of you explain what I just saw? Those were foxes. And fox-hounds. And you made the holes big enough for the foxes but too small for the hounds. How did they get inside that fence anyway?"

"They're trucked in," Amy said. She drank some of the water Jon had set before her. "They're penned up. There's no way for them to escape. And then hunters bring their hounds here for field trials. It's how they train the hounds to hunt foxes, by letting them run down foxes with no way to escape. That's how they teach the dogs to kill."

"I've heard about this," Jon said. "And I agree with you, Amy. It's inhumane. A deplorable practice. The owner of the hunt farm charges about $25 per dog. He admits ten or twelve dogs and makes about $250. All for doing nothing."

"But who brings the foxes?" I asked. "Where do they get them?"

"Trapping is legal in this state," Jon said. "It's a cowardly way for anyone to make a living but some do. Rednecks. Uneducated. Trained to do nothing but set out traps for helpless animals to wander into. Other animals get caught in their traps and often die before they're found and turned loose. Dogs and cats. Domestic pets.

"The foxes they trap that aren't good enough for the fur industry get sold for this. Brought to penned fox hunt farms, or 'canned hunt' farms as they're sometimes called."

Amy said, "But while trapping is legal, the transporting of wild animals is illegal. I've been fighting those buzzards over there ever since I moved back home. And I won't stop until I win," she declared as if there could be no other outcome. "I'll free every single fox they put over there."

"But who's responsible?" I asked. "Who owns that farm? Who's behind this?"

Amy lifted her head and smiled a mirthless smile. "That pompous ass, Buddy Henry. The hypocrite."

"Buddy Henry? The state senator?"

"None other than our holier-than-thou, swindles old people out of their land, state senator."

3

After dinner that evening, we snapped the babies' infant seats into the second row bucket seats in the Escalade. Then we loaded the double stroller, diaper bag, tote bags, and jackets into the back of the roomy SUV.

I had still not calmed down over what I had witnessed that afternoon. We never did examine the house. We decided to inspect the house another time. Amy was not in the mood. Neither were we. And it just didn't seem like a good time to bring up the subject of genealogy and inquire if we were indeed related. Nor did we stop at St. Philip's Church before returning home.

We discussed the ugly confrontation on the drive back to town, and Jon repeated what he knew about the inhumane and cruel practice of penned fox hunting. Then we decided to drop the subject, to try to salvage what was left of our day.

After being exposed to the ugly side of human nature, all I wanted was to get home to my wholesome babies and take a nap with them.

Piling baby equipment into the SUV, Jon said, "It's a good thing we didn't trade the Escalade for a smaller vehicle, even though it was something we seriously considered doing." While we wanted to support a green environment, with twins we needed the larger vehicle.

At six o'clock it was already dark but the temperature was mild for late November. Otherwise, I'd never have taken my babies out in the night air. They were wide awake but quietly sucking on their pacifiers, as if in patient anticipation of a fun evening.

"Do you think they know they're off on their first adventure?" I asked Jon as he shifted gears into reverse and we backed out into Nun Street.

"I'm sure they sense something is different. They're our kids after all so you know they're smart."

"And brave and handsome like their daddy," I said, and let my hand trail up the inside of his thigh.

Jon glanced my way and gave me that special smile he reserves for me alone. "Keep that up and you can forget about going to see the Christmas lights. I'll pull back up into the driveway and unpack this vehicle faster than you can say Airlie Gardens."

I gave his thigh a squeeze. "Later," I promised. "I had a nice nap with the twins. I feel rested and ready for anything."

I turned on our XM Sirius radio to the Broadway station. My children have displayed a decided preference for show tunes, something they inherited from their Aunt Scarlett I supposed. We drove out Oleander listening to Gene Kelly singing "Almost Like Being in Love" from Brigadoon. I have to confess to being partial to show tunes myself.

Two police officers directed traffic outside the gates at Airlie Gardens. In no time at all, we drove through the gates, handed out our tickets to the attendant, and followed his directions to the parking area. But unloading took some doing, and then getting the twins transferred into their Eddie Bauer side-by-side stroller required unsnapping their car seats from the car, then re-snapping the seats into the stroller. But our golden boys did not fuss. Eyes wide, they seemed enthralled with all the excitement going on around them.

As prearranged, we met Melanie and Cam, and Aunt Ruby and Binkie under the Airlie oak. Spotlights illuminated the huge, ancient live oak tree that dripped with Spanish moss. Experts believe the famous oak began life as an acorn sometime around the year 1545. That would have been about twenty years after Giovanni da Verrazano made landfall on the North Carolina coast just several miles from Airlie in the area that is now known as the Landfall community.

Airlie's sixty-seven acres of gardens were decorated for Christmas with thousands of brightly colored lights shaped into very tall Christmas trees. There was an indigo blue Christmas tree next to a bright red tree. Some were gold, some were bright green. In the blackness of the night, the trees stood out vividly. Many families were out enjoying the mild evening, partaking of our town's first Christmas event.

Cam and Jon walked on ahead with Jon wheeling the stroller. Every once in a while the buzz of their deep manly voices interspersed with the cooing and gurgling of my babies drifted back to my ears. My heart thrilled with happiness. My boys were having a good time – the big ones with their deep throated voices, and the little ones with their soft baby mewling.

Melanie, Aunt Ruby, Binkie and I trailed along behind the boys. But Melanie knows just about everyone, and we made slow progress as she was stopped by her many friends in the real estate business. They too were out with their families, observing this time-honored Christmas tradition.

"Oh my stars, look at that," Aunt Ruby cried. "It's a frog – a Christmas frog." On a stone path sat a frog made of bright green lights and wearing a red stocking hat.

Binkie pointed. "And just see the palm trees."

There in the distance were two palm trees, their trunks crafted of golden lights, their palm branches made of green.

The property known as Airlie was part of a 640-acre land grant from King George II in 1735. A little less than two centuries later, in 1901, Sarah Jones, wife of Pembroke Jones, created the formal gardens. The Joneses were wealthy industrialists well-known for their exuberant entertaining and love of lavish parties. Tales of Mrs. Jones' inventiveness include a party where she had platforms erected in the live oak trees. Guests enjoyed dinners in the tree tops on tables set with fine linens and china. Famous entertainers such as The Great Caruso came to entertain Sarah and Pembroke's friends who traveled to Wilmington from Newport and New York by private railroad car. Many believe the expression, "Keeping up with the Joneses," originated with Sarah and Pembroke Jones. And why would it not, given their flair for the dramatic.

Today Airlie is owned and operated by New Hanover County but the thousands of azaleas and camellias planted by Mrs. Jones still bloom and thrive.

I grabbed my camera from my shoulder bag. This was my babies' first Christmas outing and I wanted to get some photos of the little darlings before they fell asleep – or worse, began to howl.

We passed through an outdoor room where a very authentic- looking Santa Claus was thrilling the youngsters. I had Jon stand near him with the stroller and I was able to get some great shots that included my boys and the Santa.

"In a few years, they'll be up there on his knee," I said to Jon and kissed him on the cheek just because I was so happy. Then he was off, forging ahead with the stroller and Cam.

We wound around curving paths in the darkness. Silky, warm air wafted in from the ocean. The sky was clear and black and dotted with brilliant stars.

We reached one of the Airlie lagoons where out on the water a musical light show reflected on the water. People crowded the banks of the lagoon to see the musical display of sail boats and a surfin' Santa, all made of wires and tiny colorful light bulbs. But the crowd was good spirited, kind and courteous. It was a nice crowd, very family oriented, no jostling. Jon and Cam did not attempt to push the stroller to the water's edge but the others in our little party moved forward when our turn came.

"Oh, look at that," Melanie called excitedly, her arm reaching out. And then, without warning, she was lurching forward. She was pitching head first toward the water, her arms flailing as she struggled to regain her balance, and she cried out in alarm.

Binkie who was nearest to her on her left side seized her left arm and broke her fall. I grabbed onto the back of her jacket and together we stabilized her and prevented her from plunging into the lagoon.

She reared back and regained her balance. When her breath returned, she cried, "Somebody pushed me!"

"Oh, Melanie," I protested, "this crowd is really nice, very courteous. No one is pushing."

Still I wheeled about to stare at those standing behind us. A girl of about ten stood behind Melanie, waiting her turn to move to edge of the lagoon. "Is she all right?" the child's mother asked me.

Melanie turned swiftly, appraising the child and her mother. "Someone pushed me," Melanie insisted.

The woman gave her a look of alarm. "Well, it wasn't us!"

"I know that," Melanie snapped. "But did you see who it was?"

The woman grew puzzled, sliding her arm around her daughter protectively. "No," she said defensively. "Although there were some people standing in front of us but they moved away right at about the time you cried out."

"What did they look like?" Melanie demanded.

The woman appeared dumbfounded. "Just people. Ordinary people like everyone else."

She regarded Melanie critically, perhaps wondering if Melanie had been drinking. Or at the very least, was she over-reacting? "Come on, Emily," she said, taking her daughter's hand and propelling her to the front row to take our places.

Stepping away, we gathered our group together and walked back to the main path. Cam cuddled Melanie and kissed the top of her head. "You're all right, sweetheart. No harm done."

Melanie stopped in her tracks and declared in a loud voice, "I know what I felt. I distinctly felt someone's hands on my back. And then they gave me a hard push."

She turned to Binkie. "I'm glad you caught me when you did, Binkie. Otherwise I'd have fallen into the water and that bank was steep."

"I'm happy I was there for you, Melanie," Binkie responded, giving her a reassuring hug. "The ground was slippery. We should take that into account. Why would anyone want to hurt you?"

"Why indeed?" Melanie demanded, angry and puzzled. "You believe me, don't you, sis?"

"Of course," I said. But I did wonder. I had been standing on her right side and I hadn't seen a thing. But then my attention had been riveted on the light show out on the water.

As we trailed along the path, somewhat dispirited now, Binkie and Aunt Ruby bringing up the rear, he said to her in a low voice, "She pitched forward so suddenly, I don't see how she could have done that on her own. Perhaps someone did push her. Someone with a malicious streak."

And as if sensing that the mood had turned nasty, my babies began to howl.

4

"We just love the Holiday Flotilla," Aunt Ruby called from the far rear of the car on Saturday evening. "How like our dear Melanie to plan this party for all of us."

We were packed in our SUV once again, driving out Oleander to the Waterway with two fussy infants strapped into their car seats in the second row, and Aunt Ruby and Binkie seated in the third row seats that could be folded flat or upright as need dictated.

"I have someone I want you to talk to about your Revolutionary War ancestor," Binkie called over the whining of the children.

"Who is that?" I asked, almost shouting to be heard. Jon and I had made a decision that the babies' fussing was not going to curtail adult conversation. The motion of the car would soon lull them to sleep. Or so I hoped.

"My former graduate assistant."

Binkie is Benjamin Higgins, Professor Emeritus at

UNCW's history department. And husband to my deceased mother's older sister, Ruby Chastain.

"Roger Craighead's field is the Colonial period in Southeastern North Carolina. He'll be able to assist you by researching Samuel Wood for you."

I turned toward the back of the car. "I had intended to talk to Amy Wood about this but we didn't get the chance. Do you think your colleague would be willing to help?"

Jon concentrated on his driving, trying to tune out the fretting from the backseat. "Go to sleep, boys," he called authoritatively over his shoulder. The whining only got louder. When one cried, the other one joined in. Their misery seemed to feed off each other's.

And then all of a sudden, the wailing stopped. Pure, blessed silence filled the car.

"Finally," Jon said, his last nerve chewed to shreds. Mine too.

Binkie picked up the thread of the conversation. "Roger will do it if I ask him. If it were not for me, he would not have been granted a faculty position. He owes me and he knows it. Not that he isn't qualified in his field. Published, you know. But my recommendation was instrumental to his appointment. He's a hard worker and ambitious."

Binkie had furthered the careers of many young historians.

"Bring him over for drinks one evening next week," I invited. Although I could not partake of cocktails, not while nursing, that did not prevent me from entertaining others, which I heartily enjoy doing.

We turned right onto Airlie Road, then got caught in the traffic jam outside the entrance to the Airlie Gardens Christmas light show. But it didn't take long and soon we were through and on our way, passing the service road to the gardens. We drove past the turn off for Bradley Creek Road, then hung a sharp right into Melanie's private driveway where we cruised alongside the Intracoastal Waterway. Ahead, the lodge rose up in the black night, illuminated by spotlights that highlighted the square Italianate tower.

Already many of the guests had arrived but the parking valet had saved us a spot at the front door, having been instructed by Melanie that we had babies and their accoutrements to unload. Two white marble Great Danes guarded the lodge's entrance, each now decked out in whimsical red stocking hats. Cam, dressed in a thick pullover sweater, was watching for us and came bounding out to greet us and to help carry the little darlings, now blessedly sound asleep, into the lodge.

Melanie had specified casual dress. Suited me just fine because about all I can get into these days are sweat suits. My pants require elastic waists and my tops have to be stretchy to accommodate my full breasts. When I get discouraged about my figure, Jon encourages me, assuring me my waist will soon dwindle to its former small size. And my breasts? Well, he's a man, isn't he?

So to make it through this plump period, I purchased a few pretty sweat suits – happy colors and nicely designed in plush fabrics like velour and the softest cotton knit. With makeup and jewelry and ballerina flats, I didn't look too bad for a sleep-deprived, strung-out, new mommy.

I followed Cam and Jon inside, strolling over flagstones through the great arched entrance into a reception hall that extended past a broad oak staircase and led back to the Waterway side of the house. Garlands of greenery were draped from the far corners of the hall to the center of the ceiling, capping an enormous wrought iron chandelier.

The house was festive and full of people; merry voices filled the rooms, laughter, conversations, holiday music in the background. I smiled to myself. A party! I love parties.

Melanie and Cam's home is an old hunting lodge that was built during the Gilded Age of the late nineteenth century. Jon and I restored it last year, completing the project in time for us to hold our double wedding reception here. We had outdone ourselves with this restoration, if I do say so myself. The old lodge had been falling apart. Holes in the roof that let in rain. Anybody with a truck, a screw driver, and the inclination could drive up the overgrown lane and raid the place of irreplaceable valuables. And many had felt the inclination. It took Jon and me and two teams of craftsmen almost a year to bring things back to close to their original state.

But now it was perfect. Better than the original.

The two Lindas came out to welcome us: Linda Linares, the party planner, who put this event together, and Linda Price who had decorated.

"Oh, Linda, I love your decorations," I said. "And your new hair cut."

Linda ruffled her short hair with her fingers and smiled. "I decided to go with the Biltmore House theme since Melanie's lodge is from the same period and looks so much like Biltmore."

"Well, everything looks perfect," I said. "Where have my babies disappeared to?"

Linda Linares replied, "Melanie asked me to hire a sitter. And even thought it was last minute I managed to hire a college student from the University. She'll watch your babies in one of the upstairs bedrooms. Your husband and Cam are on their way up there now with the babies."

"Oh, good," I sighed. "Now I can relax and enjoy the party."

Linda Linares led me into the drawing room where huge Christmas trees filled the far two corners.

"Wherever did Linda Price find those tall trees?" I wondered aloud. The ceiling in the drawing room is sixteen feet high and the trees just about reached the top.

Linda Linares beamed. "I don't know. The girl's a wizard. Ooops, duty calls. Gotta go."

Where was Melanie? I still had not seen our hostess. Just then she came into the drawing room, dressed in a pair of beautifully tailored and fitted black slacks, black croc high heels, and a red cashmere sweater set with a string of pearls. Not all redheads can wear bright red but Melanie can. Melanie can get away with just about anything!

Melanie was escorting a man from group to group, introducing him to everyone as if he were a celebrity. There was something familiar about the man. I had seen him before but couldn't quite place him.

"Oh, there you are, shug," Melanie called, heading my way, the mystery man in tow.

He was about sixty, and his style was straight out of the Fabulous Fifties: Buddy Holly horn rim glasses, Gary Moore crew cut and bow tie. All of a sudden I knew who he was.

"Ashley, I'd like you to meet one of our state's most important senatorial leaders, Senator Buddy Henry. Senator Henry is an ally of realtors and developers especially here at the coast." Then Melanie prompted me with a little nudge of her elbow, not trusting that I would make the correct association. "Ashley's one of your biggest fans, Buddy. She's always saying how proud the folks of Brunswick County must be to have you for their state senator. Don't you always say that, shug?"

Senator Henry stuck out his hand and what could I do but shake it. "Nice to meet you, Ashley. You must be proud of this lady here. I'm looking forward to working with her as soon as she takes over the NCAR in January." He beamed at Melanie. "Between the two of us, we're going to get some much needed projects off the drawing board and into the money column."

I wondered what projects he was referring to. Melanie had said nothing to me, but then probably she would not have. Henry was much too conservative for my tastes, one of those politicians whose philosophy was that big business could regulate itself, that a free market place would ensure they operated ethically, not cut corners, preserve the environment, pay workers more than minimum wage, yada yada. I didn't buy into his flimflam. Either he was very, very naive, or the developers had bought, paid for, and now owned his soul.

I already knew enough about him to feel glad he did not represent my district. Wait until I get Melanie aside, I told myself, I'll give her an ear full about the cruel enterprise Senator Henry is operating on rural farmland.

Eager not to get into a political discussion with him, I gave Melanie a hug. "Where's Spunky? I've seen nothing of him."

"Oh, off hiding somewhere."

I turned to the senator. "Spunky is Melanie's cat. Our family are great animal lovers." I almost glared at him as I said, "Domestic pets. Wildlife. We defend them against predators. Two-legged predators, if you catch my drift."

Henry gave me an odd look. Then, ever the politician, he said, "I'm an animal lover myself. I raise dogs."

I stared him down. Not knowing where I was headed, he dropped his eyes. "Hunting dogs? That's what I heard. Do you hunt, Senator Henry? Are you a sportsman?" I emphasized the word 'sportsman.' "Because, you know, there is nothing sporting about hunting animals that have no means of escape. Don't you agree? A vile practice, I'd say."

Henry cleared his throat. Then lifted his glass to his lips and took a swallow. Then another. He'd been nursing that drink. Now he needed it.

"Ashley, what are you talking about?" Melanie asked, clearly irritated. "Oh, look, there's Katie Brinkley. Come on, Buddy, you must say hello to her." And taking him by the arm, she steered him away from me. The look she gave me over her shoulder was hostile. I'd hear about this later.

Faye Brock, Melanie's gorgeous realtor friend came by and stopped. "The decorations are fabulous. And this house! Ashley, you and Jon restored this lodge so beautifully. I've got a historic property listed in Carolina Heights and I'm going to recommend you to do the restorations."

"Thanks, Faye. Jon and I adore Carolina Heights. We'd love an opportunity to work there again." I was happy to see Faye but still smarting over my exchange with Henry.

"Well, I've gotta run. I'm going on to Kay and "Shack" Shackelford's flotilla party on Harbor Island."

"Have a good time," I called.

No sooner had Faye left than Melanie roared up to me practically foaming at the mouth. "Why are you always embarrassing me with people I'm trying to impress?"

"Why are you always trying to impress lowlife people? And where is the fox murderer senator? Better not let him near Spunky. He'd find a way to use him as bait."

"Fox murderer? Bait? What are you talking about?"

"Melanie! Hi!" A woman joined us, giving Melanie a hug.

Melanie was all smiles. "Regina! How are you, sweetie?" She exchanged air kisses with the woman. "Regina, I'd like you to meet my sister Ashley. Or have you two met?"

"I don't believe I've had the pleasure," I said. "Melanie has so many fascinating friends, I'm just getting to know them. Some too well." I gave Melanie a chilly look.

Melanie ignored me. "Sis, this lovely lady is Regina Redfield. She's very active in the NCAR. She's also a president-elect."

We shook hands. Her bony hand belied a steely grip. Regina was model skinny, not an ounce of fat on her. But stylish. Very, very stylish, in a mannequin sort of way. She wore a scarlet taffeta fitted jacket, tied at the waist, with a peplum ruffle, over black silk pants. Guess this outfit was her interpretation of the term "casual."

Melanie was babbling. "Regina's term as president follows mine the year after next. We've served on oodles of committees together, haven't we, Regina sweetie?"

Melanie slipped an arm around Regina's miniscule waist. "You couldn't have a better person on your side. Especially when you get into some of the dog fights we get into with the General Assembly. With Regina at your side, a girl can't go wrong."

"And God help the people who get in our way," Regina laughed. "We make a formidable team."

"Yes, we do." Melanie flashed her broad, disarming smile.

Regina laughed. "Grind them under our high heels, don't we Melanie?"

Melanie giggled.

"I've heard a lot about your agency." I told Regina. The Redfield Agency was big in Wilmington, with an office on South College Road and a branch office in Southport. They were developers as well as brokers and were currently developing a marina at Southport.

"Your sister is going to do us up proud. She'll make the best president the NCAR has ever seen. I can't wait to see how she shakes up this state."

Regina gave me a wide but forced smile, exposing a mouthful of brilliant white teeth. Very expensive cosmetic dentistry. A perfect small straight nose. And a very expensive hair style. Her hair was expertly tinted a soft shade of caramel, and fluffed up into a bouffant style. Not a single strand was out of place.

Then I noticed the cords in her neck. They stood out like ropes. She was scrawny, painfully thin. And flat chested. And while the latest fashions might look good on a size zero figure, I couldn't help but think her husband or lover must be mighty disappointed when she disrobed.

Just then Cam entered the room, looked around, then made a bee line for me. "How's it going up there?" I asked, referring to the nursery.

"Jon sent me to find you. He left the diaper bag in the car and he couldn't find his keys. He said he must have handed them to you."

I dug around in my bag and sure enough found the car keys which I removed and dangled. "Yep, got them."

Cam stretched out his palm to take the keys. "I'll run out . . ."

"No you won't, Cam," Melanie said. "Let Ashley do that. I've been looking all over for you, sweetie. I've got some important people for you to meet." Melanie appeared annoyed with her husband. And with me.

Regina looked from one of us to the other, picking up on the undercurrent that charged among us.

"I'll get the bag," I told Cam, and hurried out of the drawing room and into the reception hall. I glanced up the stairs. Jon must be frantic up there without clean diapers. And lord knows, my little boys sure do go through the diapers faster than Kyle Petty used to zip around a race track.

Outside, the air was fresh and cool. The dark night felt soothing after bright lights and loud voices. The valet was nowhere in sight, perhaps taking a supper break in the kitchen.

Our Escalade was the only car parked in the circular driveway. I hurried to the SUV, clicked the remote, and lifted the hatch back. Now where was the diaper bag? I didn't see it anywhere in the rear compartment. I slammed the hatch shut and went around to the second row door, opened it, and stuck my head inside.

There it was, on the floor of the back seat. I lifted it out and closed the car door. I was just starting around the car toward the entrance when loud voices stopped me. Two men stepped out of house, and from the ferocity of their voices, they were quarreling. Uh oh, this could be embarrassing.

I drew back to the far side of the Escalade, waiting for them to move away so I could have a clear shot across the driveway. But they didn't move. They were in each other's faces, so intent on their quarrel they were oblivious to my presence. I hung back. I could see them clearly in the *faux* gaslights on either side of the entrance. One of the men was Buddy Henry. The other man I'd never seen before.

"I never agreed to that," Henry was shouting, "so don't go putting words in my mouth. My constituents would throw me out of office if I was stupid enough to introduce such a bill."

The other man cursed, calling the senator the most vile names - names I am much too ladylike to repeat but not too ladylike to enjoy hearing being hurled at the fox-murderer. Then he yelled, "After all the money I've invested in you, you'd better sponsor that bill if you know what's good for you. And you'll see that it gets passed too. There won't be another penny until you do." He jabbed his finger into Henry's lapel.

Henry swiped at the man's arm, knocking it away. "Take your hands off me. Who do you think you're threatening?

You're out of your league, Red. I don't think you know who you're playing with here. I'm not some crooked county commissioner you can buy. You just try to bring me down and you'll regret it. These are state politics you're messing in, not local. Now that's the end of it. I won't do it and that's final."

And with that Senator Henry wheeled about and stomped back through Melanie's front door.

The other man, the man he'd called "Red", let out a string of curses, spat angrily at the ground, then he too returned to the party.

I scurried across the circular drive, toting the diaper bag, and prayed my entrance would not be noticed by either man.

5

I didn't see either man as I hurried across the reception hall and rushed up the broad staircase. I wandered along the upper hallway, following the sound of my babies crying. My sons are fastidious little beings and don't appreciate soiled diapers. Racing into the makeshift nursery, I attempted to hand the diaper bag to the young woman I found there. A pretty young thing of about nineteen who was able to tune out my babies' cries because she was staring at my husband with blatant and ardent desire. So smitten was she, anyone could see it written all over her face. My children were forgotten by their sitter. My husband was the object of her adoration.

Jon was sitting in a rocker, holding a bawling infant in each arm, and totally oblivious to the girl's horniness. She looked like she might, at any moment, leap onto his lap along with Peter and Jonnie.

"Thank God," Jon cried when he saw me. "I was about to mount a search party for you."

"Oh, were you?" I asked indignantly, mad at him for arousing the sitter's maidenly yearnings, although knowing Jon he was totally unaware that he was the object of her sexual fantasies.

I thrust the diaper bag at her and she had no choice but to grab it. "You're the sitter, right? There are clean diapers in there. Once you change the baby's diapers, they'll quiet down. I think you can manage on your own. You *have* changed a diaper before, haven't you?"

"Oh, yes ma'am, I have." Her blonde ponytail bobbed up and down.

Ma'am? At twenty-seven I had become a ma'am!

Her wide blue eyes peered at me innocently as if to deny what I had clearly seen.

Jon stood up and carried the babies to a make-shift changing table that had been set up on a dresser top. "Thank god you're here with clean diapers. I'll just stay and help Angelina. Be sure she has everything she needs."

Oh you will, will you, I wanted to bark. But I did not. Jon had no idea that what this quivering teenager thought she needed was him. Then I quickly reminded myself that Jon is a wonderful father. He wanted to be sure our children were being properly cared for. And so did I.

I gazed at Jon as he began undressing one of the babies. Which one? I'd have to get closer to identify my child. This attitude of mine was absurd. I trust Jon. I moved forward and began undressing the other baby. Jonnie. Little Jonnie looked up at me and began to coo. I kissed his tiny forehead. Side by side, Jon and I replaced soiled diapers with fresh. Horney Angelina was forgotten.

"Come on down and join the party," I said to Jon. "She can take over from here."

Jon lifted Peter to his chest. "I think I'll stay for a few minutes. I'll rock them and they'll be off to sleep. Then I'll be down. You go on and have some fun." He kissed me on the forehead.

"Okay," I said, smiling up at him. We were tight - a strong family unit. No blonde home wrecker could break us up. "Don't be long."

Downstairs, more guests had arrived, and I looked around for someone I knew.

"Now that's what I call a silver cougar," a familiar voice said over my shoulder.

"Aunt Ruby?" I turned to give my elegant aunt a grin. Aunt Ruby is now seventy-three but you'd never know it. She colors her hair a warm brown, eats healthy foods, and walks two miles every day, rain or shine.

"Who's a silver cougar?" I asked, amused by my aunt.

"Over there." She nodded in the direction of a man across the room.

I looked where she was staring at the man she thought was a silver cougar. He was the same man I had seen jabbing an angry finger into Senator Henry's lapel. But even though Aunt Ruby had got her appellations confused, she was right. Here in the light I could see that he was a hunk. About mid-forties. Trim yet masculine, exuding sensuality. His premature silver hair was thick and full, contrasting attractively with his black brows and flashing black eyes.

"He's got testosterone by the gallons," I said. Not some-one the older senator should be taking on.

"Bet he has a hard time keeping his zipper up," Aunt Ruby declared.

"Aunt Ruby!" I cried with fake indignation. But I was giggling too. My aunt was something.

"Don't be shocked. I've had seventy years of observing men. I know a cougar when I see one. Why do you think I chose darling Binkie Higgins to marry?"

"Aunt Ruby, you slay me. But I think cougar is meant to refer to a mature woman who is hot. Like you, my dear auntie. I believe you mean he is a silver fox. But who is he? Do you know?"

"I don't but let's find out," she said and started off. "If he was raised right, he'll be courteous to an old lady."

"Old lady, my eye," I giggled to myself as I trailed along behind my aunt.

She walked straight up to the hunky man in the tight jeans and fisherman's knit sweater. "Such a pleasant party," Aunt Ruby said to him. "I'm Ruby Chastain Higgins, Melanie's aunt."

I moved to her side, squeezing in between her and Mr. Hunk. "And this is Melanie's sister, Ashley Wilkes."

Mr. Hunk shifted his drink to his left hand and gave Aunt Ruby his right. "It's a pleasure, Mrs. Higgins. I'm Wren Redfield. One of Melanie's realtor friends."

For someone who had just come out on the short end of the stick in an angry quarrel with a state senator, he had certainly composed himself quickly. He was suave and as Aunt Ruby had predicted exhibited perfect manners.

"I think I met your wife earlier," I said. "Regina is your wife, isn't she?"

"I am," Regina said pleasantly, appearing from out of nowhere, then taking possession of Mr. Hunk by linking her arm through his.

"They're coming!" someone shouted from outside.

The flotilla was underway. The staging area for fancifully decorated fishing boats and pleasure craft was located nearby at the Bradley Creek Marina, practically at Melanie's back door.

Along with the other guests, I rushed out to Melanie's patio. I cast about for Jon, pleased to find he was there and had saved us a chaise lounge under the pergola. Big enough for two. "Hey there, handsome," I greeted, ruffling his hair. "Let me squeeze in there with you."

He looked up at me and grinned. "Sorry, Miss, but I'm saving this seat for the mother of my children."

I squeezed in between his legs and leaned back against his chest. As I rested my arms on his muscular thighs I almost couldn't blame the sitter for having designs on him. I couldn't wait to get him home. "Isn't this cozy. You make a mighty fine cushion, sir."

The flotilla sailed up the Intracoastal Waterway so close I felt I could reach out and touch the brightly lit ships. "Oh, look, here they come," I cried.

No matter how often I watch the holiday flotilla, I still get a charge when the first ship comes into view. Everyone was cheering, happy voices rising to greet the Captains and their crews.

A sailboat floated by, its mast decorated as a tall red candle, with the words "Peace on Earth" spelled out in bright green lights on its hull.

There were exclamations of pleasure, oohs and aahs from the guests on the patio and in folding chairs out on the grassy bank. I noticed that strangers had gathered some distance away on the bank overlooking the water. Finding good spots to view the flotilla can become a real challenge. It seemed that people had driven up Melanie's lane, parked in the grass, and made their way to the water. Well, why not, I wondered. Everyone loves the flotilla.

A large vessel came by showing off Santa and his sleigh and reindeer flying across the mast. All done in colorful electric lights.

There were pirate ships with crew members dressed in pirate garb, a huge inflatable Snoopy, and an entire ship done up like a whale.

But my favorite was a sail boat that was decorated to look like a huge Santa's head topped with a tall red cap.

When they reached the drawbridge the fleet would sail east through Motts Channel. The judges waited at the reviewing stand at the Blockade Runner's marina at Wrightsville Beach where the ships would be judged for awards. The entire flotilla would then float the length of Banks Channel to the Coast Guard Station near Masonboro Inlet.

I lost count of the ships that sailed by, most with Christmas music piping out to us. "This is the best flotilla yet," I told Jon.

"You say that every year," he laughed.

"I mean it every year. It just gets better and better. Oh good, now the fireworks. I don't know which part I like best."

Jon kissed the top of my head. "You're like a kid, Ashley."

"'Tis true. I am."

I nestled against him and watched the spectacular aerial fireworks display out on the water. There were fireworks shaped like peonies and dahlias and my favorite, the spiders. As they neared the grand finale, I said to Jon, "I hope this noise doesn't wake the babies. I'm going to run upstairs and check on them. That sitter was kind of flakey."

"I'll do it," he said, and began to shift me forward so he could get up.

"No, you stay and be comfy. It's my turn. Be right back."

I hurried into the house and down the hallway toward the front and into the formal reception hall. At the grand staircase I grabbed the ornately carved oak newel post and turned to mount the steps. That's when I saw a man lying on the steps. A thatch of silver hair, jeans, a fisherman's knit sweater. Wren Redfield. He was lying face down. It looked like he had taken a header down the long staircase.

At the top of the stairs stood our sitter. She appeared distraught, as if she might burst into tears.

My thoughts instantly flew to my children. "Who's watching my babies?" I demanded.

She stared down at me, gazing over Redfield's prostrate form. "They're sound asleep, Mrs. Campbell. They're fine. He's . . . I heard shouting and a thud out here in the hall and came to see what happened."

Directly behind her in the upstairs hallway was a large Palladian window overlooking the Waterway. From outside came the noise of whistles, followed by bangs and crackles.

The fireworks show had reached its finale with a shower of chrysanthemums lighting up the night sky.

I scrambled up the half flight of stairs to Redfield's side. His head was twisted, turned to the side at an odd angle. Had he broken his neck?

"Is he . . .?" the sitter asked from above.

I felt his neck for a pulse. Moved my fingertips around a bit on his throat. I'm never sure exactly where the pulse should be. But I felt no pulse, not anywhere on his neck. And he did not seem to be breathing. But a trickle of blood had drained from his nose.

I looked up at Angelina, giving her a long, suspicious glare. I did not trust her. My instincts told me she was trouble. And possibly a liar. How had she heard a fall on the stairs with all the noise from the fireworks? Had she been out here at the window watching the display, ignoring my babies?

"I think he's dead. Do you have a cell phone? I don't know where I left my purse."

6

"I don't need this kind of publicity," Melanie wailed.

On Sunday morning, my family was gathered at my house, poring over the Sunday *Star-News*. My dining room smelled of fresh coffee and the Krispy Kreme donuts Cam and Melanie had picked up on their drive in from the Waterway. Aunt Ruby was out in the kitchen, scrambling eggs and Binkie was helping her.

Coverage of the holiday flotilla appeared on the front page with a color photo of the parade of ships. But the death of prominent realtor/developer Wren Redfield dominated the news reports. And of course that the accident had occurred at Melanie's house during her flotilla party had the news media spinning out of orbit.

We skipped to the Local News section where in-depth reporting of the flotilla appeared. The reporters made much of the fact that Melanie was about to be inaugurated as the president of the NCAR at a dinner-dance to be held at the new convention center. As if accidents never happen to people in public positions.

Jon took the international section and sat down at the head of the table. "Oh my gosh," he uttered.

"What?" I asked.

"Han Cheng. Remember Han Cheng?"

"How could we ever forget that man," I groaned.

Once upon a time, Han Cheng had been a client of Melanie's. He and his wife had been trying to buy a local mansion. But the deal fell through when it was discovered that Cheng was trading in ivory, a loathsome act of cruelty to endangered elephants and prohibited by international treaty. As the Fish and Wildlife officers made their way to Wilmington to board Cheng's yacht, he and the yacht disappeared in the middle of the night like a ghost ship vanishing in the fog.

"What's that dreadful man done now?" Melanie asked.

"It's not what he's done but what has been done to him," Jon replied, an astonished expression on his face. "His yacht was seized by Somali pirates. He and his yacht are being held for ransom. But the Chinese government isn't cooperating. And no one knows if his shipping company will put up the money. In fact, the Chinese government is threatening to seize his assets."

Jon shook his head. "Doesn't look good for old Han."

"I have no sympathy for that man," Melanie declared.

"Neither do I," I said.

Cam grinned. "We've got some tough women here, Jon."

"Can't say that I'm sympathetic myself," Jon said. "Man gets what he deserves."

Cam said, "It always amazes me how the universe renders justice. You think some lowlifes are getting away with their lowlife deeds, then you learn that their histories have caught up with them."

"I sure wish the Fish and Wildlife agency would do something about the blood sport of penned fox hunting," I muttered.

Everyone at the table had heard me venting about that subject for days.

Melanie pushed the State and Local news section away in disgust. Cam picked it up and flipped through the pages idly. "I see the gaming industry is looking for ways to get around the ban on video sweepstakes parlors."

Our General Assembly had added a ban on video sweepstakes parlors to the ban on video poker games in an attempt to save gambling addicts from their own weaknesses and financial ruin.

"Just so they don't take away our lotto tickets," Cam said with a grin.

Melanie's cell phone sang to her. She took the call, wandering away from the table. "What?" she exclaimed. "You can't mean that. How was I supposed to prevent a fall?"

So someone was calling her about the accident. I had been expecting that to happen. Last night after a frantic call to 9-1-1 the EMTs arrived. They confirmed that Wren was dead. And that it appeared his neck was broken. The medical examiner had to be sent for, standard procedure in an unexplained death.

Before they arrived, I slipped past Wren's still form to go upstairs to be with my babies. I knew that once the EMTs arrived, I would be unable to use the stairs. Jon wasn't able to get by. He and I communicated by cell phone from upstairs to down. The children slept through everything. The sitter had drifted into their room, looking dazed. In spite of everything, I felt sorry for her. She was young. Had probably never seen a dead person before. While I, on the other hand, am notorious for making these discoveries, much to my dismay. I seem always to be in the wrong place at the wrong time.

She sat down on the bed and began to sob. "He came on to me."

"Who?" I cried in alarm. Was this twit about to accuse Jon of sexual harassment?

"That old man. He has gray hair. And he came on to me!"

"The dead man? What did he do?" I asked.

"He came in here and acted all friendly. And me, I like to be nice to everyone. But I sure wasn't attracted to that old man. He has gray hair!" she repeated as if gray hair meant ninety.

"What happened?"

"Well . . ." She buried her face in her hands for a moment, her blonde pony tail falling forward. Then she lifted her gaze to mine. "He kinda cornered me and tried to kiss me." She made a face of disgust. "He was slobbering all over me. I think he was drunk."

"What did you do?" I asked.

She gave me a defiant look. "I yelled at him to leave me alone. I pushed him out the door. Like, it wasn't hard to do. He was unsteady on his feet. Stumbling around. Then I closed and locked the door. Then in a little while, I heard shouting and like some thumping noises so I looked out. I thought I heard a woman screaming but that might have been like, you know, the fireworks. I . . . well, I'm sorry, Mrs. Campbell, but I remembered there was a big window in the hallway and I wanted a peek at the fireworks. You can't see them from this room. Just a little peek. I would have listened for your babies."

"So you left them?"

She looked down at her hands then shrugged her shoulders. "Just for a second. When I went out in the hall, I saw him there. Lying on the stairs. And then you came."

"I understand," I said. What was the point of arguing? "You shouldn't have left my children. But what's done is done." And you'll never sit for my children again, I vowed.

"Tell me, Angelina. Did you see anyone else around?"

She shook her head solemnly. "No one. Not a soul. Everyone was at the fireworks."

Surely the medical examiner would order an autopsy, I thought. Surely they'd at least check his blood alcohol level.

"Oh, I could just pull my hair out, I'm so mad," Melanie cried.

Cam got up from the table and went to her, put his arm around her shoulders and led her back to the table. Aunt Ruby and Binkie came in with platters of eggs and turkey bacon. "Are they tormenting my sweet girl again?" Aunt Ruby asked Melanie.

"Sit down here, babe," Cam said and pulled a chair out for her.

"What's wrong?" I asked.

"That was the chairman of the NCAR nominating committee. They have very strict standards for their presidents.

Everything has to be kosher. Why they even audited the books at my office for pity sakes. Anyway, according to her, undesirable publicity for the NCAR president reflects badly on the NCAR. Further publicity will not be tolerated. I've been warned to keep a very low profile from now on."

"But it wasn't your fault a guest fell on our stairs," Cam protested.

Melanie let her head fall onto his shoulder and let out a loud sigh. "That is precisely what I tried to explain. I've been warned, she said."

Melanie lifted her chin defiantly. "I'm inviting every realtor I know, and most definitely everyone on the nominating committee, to my Christmas party. I'll show them what Southern hospitality is all about. Then they'll love me again." She choked back a sob.

"Here, here," Binkie said.

"That's my girl," Aunt Ruby said. "You're a Chastain. From a fine old Savannah family. Who do they think they're dealing with? We'll show them. I'll help. We'll put on the best doggone party this town has ever seen."

"I've got a few chips to cash in," Cam said. "Maybe I can get a big star to come."

"That's so sweet, sugar, but you're forgetting. Scarlett will be here. She's our sister and she's a huge star."

"Grand idea," Binkie said. "Keep this in the family."

It made me so happy to see how Binkie had gone from solitary bachelor to the proud patriarch of our family.

Aunt Ruby clapped her hands. "Splendid idea. We'll have Scarlett perform for your guests. Oh, they'll love her! And you."

7

"I've been studying Wilmington's role in the Revolutionary War since I was a kid," Roger Craighead told us. "Since my first visit to Moore's Creek National Battlefield."

Roger Craighead was our guest for dinner on Tuesday evening. Aunt Ruby had made her favorite chicken and rice casserole, Melanie brought a huge salad, and Cam had baked his famous four-layer chocolate cake. The babies were down for the night – fingers crossed – and we were finishing up dessert in my dining room.

My house is 150 years old and I restored it lovingly with Jon's help. The dining room is one of my favorite rooms, papered in a red and white toile pattern with a richly colorful oriental rug placed under my mahogany double-pedestal table.

Roger continued, "Binkie said you wanted to know about the Wood family and I know a great deal about them. You think you might be related to them?"

"We're not sure," Melanie said.

"What makes you think you might be?" he asked.

"A will we recently found among our parents' possessions," I said.

Roger's eyes lit up with interest. "Ah, family wills offer a wealth of information. Children's names, spouse's names, where the deceased lived. And of course what he owned. Or she."

Roger was in his early thirties, fair complected with sandy colored hair and wore prescription glasses. He was dressed in jeans and a striped shirt, sleeves rolled up to mid-forearm. A pleasant man, soft-spoken and composed. "May I see the will?"

"Certainly," Melanie said and handed him a large manila envelope across the dinner table.

Aunt Ruby got up and began removing plates and cutlery. I got up to help her. "No, you sit, Ashley. Benjamin will help. Besides you'll want to hear what Roger can tell you about your ancestors."

"Why don't we move into the library?" Jon suggested.

So we gathered up our coffee cups and napkins and moved down the hall into our spacious red library. Three years ago my house had been on the Candlelight Tour. I'd decorated five Christmas trees for my house. Was I going to regret not having even one this year?

Settled on one of the matching leather sofas, Roger opened the envelope eagerly and withdrew a single large folded sheet of paper. Quickly he scanned the sheet.

"Is this all?" he asked. "Only one page?"

Melanie looked at the paper in his hand, looked into the envelope, and shook her head. "I don't know where my mind is these days. There was another page that listed signatures of witnesses but somehow I left it at home."

Roger gave her an odd look.

Cam gave her an odd look too, blinked, then got it.

I did too. Melanie had deliberately left out the page that referred to the Wilmington treasure. My sister is not just another pretty face.

"And that was all?" Roger asked.

"Yes," Melanie replied. "The first page tells that he left his land to his son David."

"Let me have a quick read," Roger said.

The first page of the will named Samuel Wood, his daughters by name, and his son David by name. Sufficient for genealogical purposes.

Roger read the single page slowly. "Yes, here he bequeaths his land to his son. You know, this is a real find. This document is a copy of the original will that was made at the same time the will was signed. Not having copy machines or computers, those folks had scribes to hand-copy important documents. And it is lucky that you have this copy because a fire in the basement of the old county courthouse in Southport destroyed many documents of this era. Yes, you are very lucky."

"What can you tell Melanie and Ashley about the will?" Cam asked. "Do you know if there is a connection between the Wood family and the Wilkeses?"

Roger pulled a folded sheet of lined paper from his shirt pocket. "I did some research this afternoon." He smiled at me and Melanie. "I can tell you exactly how you are related to the old Wood family. And it's a family to be proud of. I'll fill you in on that later.

"But first I'll tell you exactly how you are related. This isn't hard to find out if you know where to look."

"I wouldn't begin to know where to look," I said.

"Neither would I," Melanie added.

"Your father was Peter Wilkes." He smiled. "As, of course, you are well aware. Peter's mother was born Ella Humphreys. Now Ella was the daughter of a man named Albert Humphreys. Albert was the son of John Humphreys, a Civil War veteran. But Albert's mother was a Wood. Margaret Wood.

"Margaret was the son of Samuel Wood who died rather mysteriously. This Samuel was the grandson of the original Samuel Wood. It was the custom at that time for the first son to be named for his paternal grandfather. The second son would be named for his maternal grandfather. And the third son was named for his father. Unlike today, when first sons are named for their fathers with Jr. added.

"This Samuel – he would be your great-great-great-grand-father – or g3 as we like to say – was the son of David Wood. You saw that David Wood is named in the will as the primary heir of his father, of the first Samuel Wood's estate."

"It's amazing that you were able to find this information," I said.

"And you found this all out in one afternoon. I'm impressed," Melanie said.

Roger smiled with pleasure.

"Quite a bit is known about the original Samuel Wood. Much information has come to light only recently. With the advent of the internet and the digitalization of many old history books and chronicles, newspaper articles, plus state and federal archives now available online, the internet has become a treasure trove of information for researchers like me. But there are also legends that have not been confirmed."

"That is certainly true," Binkie said, coming into the library with Aunt Ruby. They settled into armchairs just as a whimper sounded from the baby monitor. We all listened intently, praying the whimper would not escalate into full-blown bawling. It did not, and we let out our breaths.

Roger seemed bemused. He was a single man consumed by his love of history.

"This is a direct quote from Lord Cornwallis: 'North Carolina is of all the provinces in America the most difficult to attack . . . on account of its great extent, of the numberless rivers and creeks, and the total want of interior navigation.'"

He went on, "If you recall your North Carolina history, after the Battle of Guilford Courthouse in modern-day Greensboro, Lord Cornwallis marched his troops south to Wilmington. Technically, Cornwallis won that battle against General Nathanael Greene but he lost a quarter of his soldiers. Cornwallis took no prisoners with him from Guilford Courthouse because they would have been too great a burden. He was already burdened with the transport of ammunitions wagons he'd captured, artillery, cannon balls, and gunpowder – supplies he badly needed.

"Colonel Tarleton's cavalry rode ahead of the main army which numbered about fifteen hundred British and German soldiers. When they reached present-day Sanford, they were ambushed by an American militia. The militia men rode directly into their ranks, thus causing them to scatter. Even so, the militia was greatly outnumbered and they suffered defeat. Some managed to escape. Many were taken prisoner and marched to Wilmington."

Binkie smiled. "I told you he was good."

"I had a good teacher," Roger said.

"This happened in 1781 and at that time, Wilmington was controlled by the Loyalists under the command of Major Craig. Lord Cornwallis commandeered the Burgwin-Wright house and set up a temporary headquarters in it. The prisoners he'd captured at Sanford were rowed out to a prison ship, the *Forby*, that was anchored in the Cape Fear River.

"Now here's where the legend comes in. For some reason that is unknown – and as I say, I have no proof that this is true – some prisoners were imprisoned in the old jail under the Burgwin-Wright house. It was no more than a dungeon. One of those prisoners was supposedly your ancestor, Samuel Wood, along with his brother-in-law James Hughes.

"Cornwallis remained at the Burgwin-Wright house for eleven days in April, from the 13th through the 24th. During that time his soldiers were outfitted with better clothing and shoes and generally used their time to rest and prepare for another march. Cornwallis used the time to correspond with Major General Phillips in Virginia. Should he follow General Greene into South Carolina and engage him there? Or should he march his Cavalry and Infantry into Virginia? He decided on Virginia."

Roger laughed. "And the rest as they say 'is history' for in October of that year he surrendered to General Washington at Yorktown."

Roger sipped his coffee. "However, according to the legend, an incident occurred at the Burgwin-Wright house before Cornwallis departed. The legendary incident involves your g5 grandfather, that would be Samuel Wood, and your g5 uncle, James Hughes."

I noticed that we all were scooching forward on our seats.

"On April 24th, the army made preparations to depart. There was much commotion as they assembled, packed supplies, prepared the wagons and the horses, and tended to everything that had to be done to march an army north across the state of North Carolina and into Virginia.

"Somehow Samuel and James managed to overcome a guard. They exchanged articles of his clothing for their own so that they could mingle undetected with the soldiers milling about Market Street.

"When darkness fell, and the soldiers were catching some shut eye in preparation for an early departure the next morning, Samuel and James managed to hitch a horse to a supply wagon. And they rode off with it. Their intent was to find and join up with General Greene and deliver the supplies to him. Once outside of town, they found a secluded place and looked through the supplies they were carrying."

"This is so exciting," I couldn't refrain from saying.

Roger continued. "If you go on the internet you will find numerous websites devoted to the belief that Lord Cornwallis left a fortune in gold in North Carolina when he marched off to Virginia."

Melanie rubbed her hands enthusiastically. "Oh goody, gold."

Roger smiled indulgently. "To continue, Samuel and James searched the supply wagon. Imagine their astonishment when they discovered a barrel containing gold. That made them even more determined to get the supplies and the gold to General Greene.

"When they stopped at villages they thought might be safe, they made inquiries about General Greene's next campaign. Remember, that while Greene was marching to South Carolina, they were prisoners of Cornwallis and on their forced march to Wilmington so they had no way of knowing that Greene was headed for Camden.

"Unfortunately, James had been wounded during the skirmish at Sanford. And his wounds only got worse so that on their journey in search of Greene and the American army, James became fevered and delirious. Then he died."

"Mercy," Aunt Ruby uttered. Binkie took her hand.

"Samuel was grief-stricken. They were like real brothers. They'd fought side by side since 1775, joining one militia after another. He was determined to bury James in the Hughes family plot in Sanford and he managed to find his way back there and to bury James in secrecy with only members of the Hughes family in attendance. Then Samuel took his young wife Elizabeth and the barrel of gold, and made his way to Brunswick County. Using some of the gold he bought himself a huge longleaf pine forest, so remote he hoped not to be found by either the Loyalists or the Americans. With James' death, he had had enough of war and simply wanted to live in peace. And in fact the war was just about over.

"Thus he settled in Brunswick County and raised a family there. This we know. He was able to make a living by supplying the naval stores industry with pitch, tar, turpentine, and lumber. But according to the legend, he did not spend any more of the gold for fear of arousing suspicions. His descendants survived and thrived. Whether they knew of the gold is unknown. The family home never changed hands. It is occupied by a Wood even now."

"Dr. Amy Wood," I exclaimed.

"Yes, Dr. Wood. Do you know her?"

"She's our babies' pediatrician," Jon answered.

"But what about the gold?" Binkie asked.

"Yes, what about the gold?" Cam seconded.

"No one knows if it ever existed. But if it did, it is well hidden because there has never been a mention of it since."

Roger chuckled. "Now if I were a gambling man, I'd say it is hidden at the bottom of a deep well, the well grown over. Unseen. Forgotten. It'll never be found."

Binkie said, "As you say, legends that Cornwallis left behind gold abound. None have ever been proved. I'm afraid this is but another fanciful tale. I sincerely doubt that gold exists. Granted, the main thrust of this story may be true. That Samuel and James made off with a supply wagon. But that the supply wagon contained gold? I sincerely doubt it."

"I don't know, Binkie," Roger said, disagreeing with his former professor. "Where there's smoke there's fire."

"I'm with Binkie," Melanie said. "If you listen to the legends there's more gold hidden in Wilmington than in Ft. Knox."

Good, I thought, throw him off the track. Still, our family had the proof that there was a "Wilmington treasure." It was listed in our g5 grandfather's will. I was with Melanie. We should show that will to no one but immediate family.

8

After lunch on Wednesday Melanie drove me out Oleander toward Bradley Creek.

"What would I do without Aunt Ruby and Binkie? I feel like I'm taking advantage of them but they are so good with my boys."

"You're not imposing. Those two just love taking care of your twins," Melanie said. "And you know, shug, this is the closest to being grandparents they'll ever get."

"Yes, that's true. But I still feel like I'm taking advantage of them."

"Aunt Ruby is forthright. She'll tell you when she's tired, or can't do it."

I yawned noisily. "Jon has a design project he's trying to finish. I ought to be at home taking a nap. Wouldn't Mama and Daddy just love to baby-sit the twins? I wish they were still with us; I miss them so much."

"Me too," Melanie said and reached over to pat my knee.

I had to admit Melanie's driving was improving. She was

getting better at keeping her eyes on the road. And she was not speeding. This improvement had to be Cam's doing.

"Mama and Daddy would have been so thrilled with grandchildren," I went on. "But, I've got to say, as much as I adore those precious babies of mine, it sure is nice to have an hour to myself."

"I figured as much. That's why I insisted on picking you up and taking you to this showing. I don't have any appointments for tomorrow so I can go shopping for furniture for the nursery I'm setting up at my house. Although I'd give anything to have another listing to show."

"Don't be discouraged, Mel. The market will pick up. And won't this one bring you a big commission?" I asked. "I wish I could get away tomorrow to shop for baby furniture with you but Jon's got an appointment so I can't get away."

"Oh, that's OK, sis. Cam will come with me. The studio isn't busy over the Christmas season and he's really eager to do this. And sure, I should earn a big commission. When it sells. If it sells. And it isn't going to be easy to sell. How many people have that kind of money?"

Melanie couldn't stop raving about the fabulous listing that had dropped into her lap.

"I don't know if I'll do any holiday decorating this year," I moaned. "I can't seem to get my head above water. I'm tired all the time. I feel like I'm walking around in a stupor. And since we're all spending Christmas with you and Cam at the lodge, there doesn't seem to be much point to dragging out my Christmas stuff. Although it's going to take a caravan to transport all the baby things we are going to need for a few days away from home."

"I've got plenty of space for everyone and for your baby equipment. The lodge is spacious. And perhaps by then I'll have a nursery set up for them."

"What a Godsend that will be. You are so great, Aunt Melanie."

She gave me a quick smile. "My pleasure."

"Melanie, about last night and Roger Craighead. You were right not to show him the page that referred to the Wilmington treasure. That would be proof that the legend is true – that Cornwallis really was transporting gold - and I don't want anyone knowing there is a possibility, no matter how remote, that the gold was spirited away by our ancestor."

"I agree. And did you ever have any idea we were related to Amy Wood?"

"Not a clue. Jon and I were discussing the situation late last night."

"So were Cam and I. We think we should keep very quiet about the will and the treasure."

"Gosh, Mel. Jon and I came to the same conclusion. We think we should be very careful about the treasure aspect of all this and not tell anyone. Not until we can find out more. I'm going to feel out Amy Wood to see if she has ever heard about a treasure. You know, I seriously doubt there is one. I think this is just another rumor."

"Cam and I were thinking along the same lines. Nobody reads that will for the time being. The only ones who know are family and none of us will talk. We don't want any discussion of this family treasure business being shared with outsiders. First of all, if there is nothing to it, we'll end up looking like fools. And if there is . . . something . . . a treasure . .

. And how odd would that be? Well, we don't need any problems in our life with . . . with, well, I don't know what. But people do strange things when something like a treasure is involved."

"My sentiments exactly," I agreed.

Melanie pulled onto a small road that ran along beautiful Bradley Creek. There were breathtaking views of the marina and the Waterway. "I can't wait for you to see this house. You won't believe it."

"Didn't you say your appointment was at two? We're late, Mel. Did I make you late?"

"Pish posh, don't worry about that. Men won't admit it but they love being kept waiting by women. Especially pretty women. Sure, he'll be stomping around, cursing, but the minute he lays eyes on us, he'll forget all about his anger."

"Humph. You and I must know different men, that's for sure." I imagined the reaming out I'd get if I stood up a carpenter or roofing contractor.

"Here's the thing, shug, this is a trustee sale so I have a small window of opportunity before my listing gets posted on the MLS. And what with the big bucks at stake, other brokers from all over the state will be storming down here to show this house. Then I'll have lots of competition, and as you know, even though I thrive on competition, when it comes to earning a big commission I intend to get this sale nailed down as tight as a coffin."

"What a ghoulish turn of phrase. How much money are we talking about?"

"The owner owes almost eight million on it. I'll mark it down to six and see what happens."

"Six million! That'll bring a pretty hefty commission." I couldn't help being very impressed. I'd seen Melanie pull off some coups in the real estate business, but if she pulled this off, it would be like winning the lottery.

"I'm glad you get it how important this listing is to me. Now if I play my cards right, and my luck holds, I'll get this baby under contract, hopefully this afternoon. Then, as the selling agent as well as the listing agent, I'll pocket the full six percent commission. I won't have to split with another realtor.

"What a holly, jolly Christmas that will be. Three-hundred-sixty thousand dollars under my tree! Noel! Noel!"

I gave my gorgeous sister a long look. "If anyone deserves a sale like this, it's you, Mel. You've paid your dues in spades. I know how hard you've worked all these years, how much good will you've spread around in the real estate community. You're a leader in the Council of Residential Specialists. You've given so much of your time to your local board. You've been voted Wilmington's sales person of the year time after time.

"I know first hand the favors you've done for a lot of folks. I'd say you're about as popular as Oprah."

Melanie gave me a big smile of gratitude. "Thanks for believing in me, little sis. I'm so lucky to have a sister like you. And a husband like Cam. He understands that I have to work 24/7. Doesn't complain. He's the same way with his production studio. We're both driven."

"You've created good karma for yourself, Melanie. Fling some largesse out there into the universe and, like a karmic boomerang, it comes caroming back to you. With interest."

At age twenty-one, Melanie had been voted Miss North Carolina, representing our state in the Miss America talent and beauty pageant. At the time, I was only thirteen. How I had adored my big sister. Still do.

"Who is your client?" I asked. "And are you sure I won't be in the way?"

"This guy is one of the few men in the state with the personal wealth to close this deal. He's Jack McAllister, CEO of Bank of USA, headquartered in Charlotte. The bank will be paying big bonuses at the end of the year. I've been showing him property out here on the Waterway for eons. But we never seem to find one that shoots off enough sparks for him. This one will do just that.

"And no, you won't be in the way. The house is enormous. Just wander around. Or trail along with us, if you like."

Melanie's new, hot-off-the-assembly-line Cadillac DTS – her slogan in these days of tough economic times is "Buy America" – cruised up the bluff. There was a circular driveway in front of the house. She parked alongside a fire-engine-red, mid-life-crisis, sporty little BMW convertible.

A nice looking man of about fifty was pacing the driveway, fussing and fuming. Melanie powered down her window and gave him a little wave. As soon as he clapped eyes on her, you could see him melt. Just like all men who come within Melanie's pheromonal radius, he was smitten.

In one long stride he reached the driver's side door and held it open for her. "Hey, Jack!" Melanie called as she slid out of the driver's seat, flashing her client a shapely thigh.

I got out on my side and ventured around the car.

"What do you think, Jack?" Melanie greeted him. "Did I exaggerate? Is this place spectacular or is it spectacular?"

A soft breeze from the water ruffled the man's thick salt and pepper, expensively coiffed hair. He wore power like a silky second skin.

The same breeze lifted Melanie's long auburn waves and she gave her head a little toss causing her hair to swing suggestively around her shoulders – a real turn on for men.

"Hey there, gorgeous," Jack crooned as he moved in to draw Melanie into a hug and to kiss her cheek.

I was invisible. How many times has this happened to me in my lifetime, I asked myself. Too many to count.

But Melanie had not forgotten me. "Jack, this is my sister Ashley. She and her husband Jon are in the home restoration business."

"Hi, Jack," I said and stepped forward to shake his hand.

"Nice to meet you, Ashley," he said.

"I hope I'm not intruding," I said.

"Not at all. A second opinion is always useful. Especially from someone in the business."

Melanie linked her arm through his and led him off. "Now, Jack, sweetie, you are the first person I thought of when I got this listing. I knew it would be perfect for you. No one has seen it yet."

Well, that was not true! On the drive out Melanie told me she had shown the house that very morning to a local wheeler-dealer. But when they'd gotten down to bottom-line figures, he had confessed to her that six mil, even five mil, was out of his reach in this recession. Besides, she had told me, he owned property that he'd have to sell first before he could buy out here.

She had sworn me to secrecy. And since I didn't even know who the early morning client had been, what was there to tell? But I couldn't help wondering why a man, who admitted he didn't have the money, and who already owned a home with land, had wanted to view the new listing in the first place. But the ways of the real estate world are a mystery to me.

"Come on, handsome," Melanie said to Jack, "let's walk out on your very own boat dock and let you see it from the water side." She turned back to me. "You too, Ashley. You won't believe this view."

She moved on ahead down a broad paved path to the private boat dock, adding a little wiggle to her walk.

Then she turned back to give Jack an inviting smile over her shoulder. "The water view of the house is what your friends will see when they pull up in their yachts for your first party. Isn't this impressive?"

Jack unlocked his gaze from her *derriere* and turned to give the house his full attention. He whistled, then nodded his head slowly. "That house is a knock-out. You weren't kidding, Mel."

His arm snaked around her waist innocently, as if enthusiasm had gotten the better of him. I moved on ahead, stepped onto the boat dock and trailed it out over the blue water.

The weather was perfect. The day was beautiful: mild temps, playful breezes, puffy little white clouds tracking a Carolina blue sky. Across the sparkling water, beyond the marshes, lay the southern end of Wrightsville Beach with its colorful beach cottages.

Turning north, I called, "Isn't that your house I see in the distance?" There was the red tile roof of Melanie's lodge peeking out of the tree tops.

"It is. We'll be neighbors, Jack."

Jack joined me at the end of the pier and we turned back to admire his maybe future house. "What's your opinion, Ashley?" he asked. "Is this worth six mil of my hard earned money?"

"I think it's magnificent. And I'd say that even if Melanie were not the listing agent. There's not enough money in the world to buy this view. It's priceless."

As his eyes roved over the impressive structure, Melanie recited some facts.

"Eighty-five hundred square feet, Jack," she said. "Three levels. A four-car garage on the lower level. Double decks on two sides. Twenty foot ceilings on the upper level."

She placed a hand on his arm and leaned into him. "And wait until you see the view of the water from that observatory." With her other hand, she pointed to a glass cupola that topped the roof like a glittering crown.

"I've got to admit, it's some house, Melanie. And we've been looking for the right house for . . . how long now?"

"Almost a year, Jack," she said pleasantly, as if she had all the time in the world for this hard-to-please man to make a decision.

He continued along his train of thought. "Now as I explained to you yesterday on the phone, with the depreciation in property values, six mil is just too much for any house. Unless it's the Taj Mahal."

Melanie turned to him and chuckled. "Who wants to live in India, Jack? While the Carolina coast is the perfect location. And you know what they say about real estate . . ."

"Location, location, location," he sang with a grin.

"Look, Jack, you're a practical business man. So am I . . ."

Jack gave her a once over. "Nobody would ever confuse you for a man, Melanie."

I smiled to myself. Okay, Melanie, I thought, enough of this flirtatious banter. If you want to sell this house, you'd better get serious and stop the flirting.

She must have read my mind because she said, "Jack, listen to me, once this recession is over – and it *will* end – inflation is going to kick in and this place will be selling for twelve mil, not six. And in about two years, a tidal wave of baby boomers is going to hit this coast like a tsunami, and the cost of nice houses is going to go through the roof. You mark my words. I attend the conferences, the workshops, where economic forecasts are laid out for us by the experts. You're one yourself. You know I'm on target here."

Jack folded his arms over his chest. His chin tipped perceptibly. "Yeah, you've got something there. Well, okay, what are we waiting for? Show me around inside."

9

We strolled off the boat dock and up the paved path that was bordered with tall, willowy sea grass swaying in the soft breeze.

"Two acres," Melanie told him. "The nearest neighbor," and she pointed to a closed-up looking house a distance away where a black pick-up truck was parked in the driveway, "lives up in New England someplace and doesn't get down here much. The perfect neighbor." She smiled sweetly at him and he returned the smile, his eyes conveying all sorts of admiration and invitations.

Mind your own business, Wilkes, I told myself.

The circular driveway was nicely landscaped and we trotted across it to mount a set of shallow flagstone steps that led to a broad sheltered front porch.

A large green Christmas wreath hung on the oversized, elaborately paneled front door. Melanie inserted a key in the lock and the front door swung inward.

"Now, isn't this a breathtaking entrance?" she asked.

I couldn't agree more. A grand staircase curved upward, following the contour of a bowed, windowed wall that overlooked the driveway.

"Look at that," I said, indicating a cat walk on the second floor that curved around in front of the upper windows.

Jack was silent, gazing, considering. He didn't have to speak. I could tell from his expression that he was as smitten with Melanie's house as he was with Melanie.

"Come on, wait till you see this," Melanie invited. Jack and I followed her lead, and strolled down a hallway that looped around to an immense open area. "Look at this, Jack. Some party room, huh? Kitchenette, lots of room for entertaining. Sliding glass doors all around."

She went to unlatch one of the doors, fumbled with it, looked puzzled, then slid the door open easily. We stepped out into the sunny November air. "The wood decking is specially treated so that it never gets hot under your bare feet in summer."

"Nice pool," Jack said, admiring the dazzling blue water of the kidney-shaped swimming pool that was surrounded by decking. "And what's that body of water over there?"

"A salt water stream," Melanie responded. "Your very own. On your very own property." She beamed at him like he was just too smart for words.

I trailed along behind them toward the Waterway side, as Melanie said, "You've got views in three directions."

To myself I thought, if the views of the incredibly breathtaking Intracoastal Waterway did not close this deal for her, short of sleeping with him, I didn't know what else she could do. This land was a little piece of heaven on earth.

"Man, there's nothing like the sight of water stretching in all directions to bring down the old blood pressure." Jack had mellowed out.

"You'll live to be a ripe old age out here," Melanie told him as she stepped back inside the house. Then she showed us the guest bedroom wing: three bedrooms, each with its own private bath and dressing room. "Guest wing, or in-law quarters, kids' quarters, however you want to use this space." She winked at him. "Take your pick; you can do a lot of swinging in this house."

"How many bathrooms altogether?" he asked, ever the executive.

Melanie considered for a moment. "Too many to count. Let's just say, you'd better stock up on the toilet paper." Her laughter was light.

I let my fingers trail over a console table under an ornate gilt-framed mirror that stood on the landing between the first and second floors. For some inexplicable reason the previous owner had left behind a few items of furniture. But I had learned enough about real estate sales from Melanie not to be surprised by the frivolous things her clients did.

"Naturally, your own furniture will be far superior to this," Melanie commented. "Shirley has exquisite taste." Shirley was Jack's wife whom he often seemed to forget existed.

We took the stairs to the top floor where there was an astonishingly huge great room full of incredible light with an adjoining open kitchen.

"The ceiling is twenty feet high" Melanie said. "And these are cork floors. This house is environmentally friendly - green. You don't know how popular that will make you with the right people. Their esteem for you will soar. The built-ins are knotty cypress but the wood is recycled, rescued from an older home that was coming down. The builder of this house is not guilty of destroying the rain forest. Your conscience can rest easy living here."

Jack leaned his tight buns against the granite-topped island that separated the kitchen from the great room.

"Now who left that there?" Melanie asked in irritation as she eyed a Starbucks paper coffee cup. "Honestly, you can't rely on anyone these days. Those sloppy house cleaners." She walked over to the offending paper cup, grabbed it up, and tossed it into a plastic-lined trash basket.

"Who was the builder?" Jack asked. "And exactly how old is this house?"

Melanie seemed not to have that information at her fingertips. "Why don't I fax the pertinent information to your office?" she suggested, and Jack nodded his assent.

"Did you say this was a foreclosure sale?" he asked.

Good question. So he was seriously interested.

"No," Melanie replied. "It's a trustee sale. A bank in Dallas owns it. The original owner fell into hard times. This is but one of his remaining assets. Man owned property all over. The bank contracted with me to appraise and sell this property. The owner owes just about eight million on it but because of this current market, we'll let it go for six."

Jack's salt and pepper eyebrows shot up on his forehead and I could see dollar signs flashing in his eyes. A deal, he was thinking to himself. Now he was wondering if he could talk her down. Na uh. Melanie had already calculated her commission.

"Follow me," she instructed. "You've never seen a house with anything like this."

She led the way up a circular staircase. Surely she knew he was gawking at her legs.

"Isn't this something!" she sang out.

"Oh, wow!" Jack exclaimed.

"Oh my stars," I said.

We were in the cupola, glass on all sides, water and small green islands as far as the eye could see. "And there's the Atlantic." Melanie pointed to glimpses of the ocean visible beyond the barrier islands.

"Okay, I've gotta admit, Melanie, this house is rare. My wife will love it. My kids will love it. And when we entertain . . . well, we'll be the envy of everyone we know."

"That's a given, Jack," she said and gazed at him so adoringly you'd have thought he was buying it for her and she was going to move in here with him.

We descended the stairs and returned to the second floor great room where Melanie contemplated his expression. Was he sold? He seemed to be to me. I scarcely breathed, afraid of saying the wrong thing.

He was grinning from ear to ear as if the word "yes" was about to slip off his tongue.

Melanie looked like she was going to break out in her cheerleader's twirl, whooping and leaping into the air. But she remained still. "This one is special, Jack. It'll go fast."

Always helps to inject a little fear.

Jack nodded slowly. He had met his match. And he was hers.

"Let's check out the master suite," Melanie said, "It's immense and there's a hot tub on a private deck off the bedroom. Just think of what that will do for your love life."

Cater to the old libido. "Then we'll talk," she said, but Jack was far away, picturing himself and a couple of topless beauties in that hot tub. Mrs. Jack would put the kibosh on that little fantasy.

Just then Melanie's blackberry played a merry tune from inside her purse. "I'd better check this," she told him. "You go on ahead. It's just around the corner and up a couple of steps." She pointed and Jack went on ahead.

I stepped over to the window wall while Melanie set her purse on the granite-topped island, digging into it for her link to the internet and the world. "I'll just check to see who this is," she told me. "Make sure it isn't someone I have to take right away."

She hadn't even clicked the phone on when we heard Jack bellow from the adjoining wing, "What the hell? Melanie, you'd better get in here!"

She raced up the short flight of steps to the master suite with me at her heels. What could be so urgent, I wondered. A water leak? Damage from vandals? My mind raced.

We found Jack standing in the center of the immense bedroom, jacket parted, fists on hips, glaring his outrage.

The room was devoid of furniture except for the king-size four-poster bed with a floral coverlet that for some reason had been left behind.

A man lay on the bed, flat on his back, fully clothed, toes of black loafers pointing heavenward.

"Is he asleep?" Melanie cried, alarmed. "And how did he get in here?"

"Asleep? With his eyes open?" Jack asked, clearly pissed at this turn of events.

I moved toward the bed. Sure enough, Jack was correct. The man's gray eyes behind his horn-rimmed glasses were wide open. But glassy. Staring unseeing at the ceiling.

"Something's wrong with him," I said. "Is he . . .?"

"Dead?" Jack finished. "I think so. Or close to it." He narrowed his eyes and fixed his gaze on Melanie. "You know who this is, don't you?"

"I'm afraid I do," she replied.

"This is not good," I said.

"That's Buddy Henry," Jack said. "State senator from Brunswick County. The man's trouble. Always has been. What the hell's he doing here?"

Melanie did not reply. I remained mute. But hadn't she confided on the drive out that she had shown the house earlier to a local wheeler-dealer. That sure described Henry.

Her blackberry was still in her hand. "I'll call 9-1-1."

"Hold on, Mel," Jack said. "I can't be here when the cops come. I can't afford this kind of publicity. Not in my position. The banks are getting enough bad press these days. The media would have a field day if they knew I was here. What would the stock holders say? What would my board of directors say? No way am I getting involved in this . . . whatever happened here."

We must have looked shocked because he went on, "Now, I'm out of here, girls. I was never here. You got it? You two came alone, checking on your listing or whatever when you found him like this."

Already Jack was starting for the door. "I like the house. You knock it down to four and a half, and we've got a deal. I'll take it off your hands. But first clear up this mess. And if you breathe a word about me being here, the deal is off."

10

While Melanie spoke to the dispatcher at 9-1-1, I called Jon. As soon as he got the full import of what I was babbling about – and yes, indeedy, I was babbling a mile a minute – he insisted on driving straight out. "I'll be there as fast as I can."

I stared at Melanie across the bed, looked at her over Buddy Henry's stricken body. He lay still, very, very still. And appeared not to be breathing. I looked for the slow lift and fall of his chest, but he was as immobile as a wooden dummy. Exactly as Redfield had looked when I found him on Saturday night. And like Redfield a small trickle of blood had congealed at his nostrils.

"Was he the one you had out here this morning?" I asked.

"Yes," she murmured, pacing, and cogitating hard.

"Well, he did leave with you, didn't he? You didn't leave him behind here in the house?"

"Of course, he left with me. I'm responsible for this house. I wouldn't permit anyone to be in here unattended. Well, that is, the cleaning service was here on Monday and

Tuesday. You can't imagine what a mess this place was. Dirty carpet, odds and ends left behind. Why the master bathroom looked like someone had simply gone out for a stroll, not moved away entirely. Shampoo bottles, prescription bottles, soap, wash cloths."

"Melanie!" I shouted.

"What?"

"You're babbling." Guess this tendency runs in the family.

"But . . . I think one of the sliding glass doors was unlocked."

"Downstairs?"

"Yes, on the main level. When I went to unlatch the door, it already was unlatched. I'm sure I locked up this morning."

"Could he . . ." and I nodded with my chin to the unconscious body on the bed "have unlatched it?"

"But why?"

"I don't know. Clearly, he got back inside somehow."

"Yes," she said thoughtfully. "He did."

In the distance I heard the wail of sirens, drawing nearer and nearer until the high-pitched screech was right under our windows, abruptly dying. "They're here."

I went out into the hall and looked down through a window to the circular driveway. A fire truck. Very quickly, four firemen jumped out of the truck and dashed up onto the porch.

"We'd better get down there and open the door before those firemen bring out the axes and chop it down."

The next thing I was aware of was being surrounded by four big burly firemen. They must have spent every free minute of their downtime hefting barbells because those guys had some serious musculature. No females on this team.

One fireman was a bit older than the other three. "Where is he?" he asked.

"Upstairs. I'll show you," Melanie replied.

"No, ma'am, you wait here. My men will handle this."

"You got it, Captain," one of the team called as the three firemen ran up the stairs two at a time while hoisting some piece of equipment with them, the purpose of which was a mystery to me.

"You say there's a state senator up there?" the captain wanted to know.

"Yes, sir," Melanie answered. She was very subdued, not her usual animated self.

"Senator Henry from Brunswick County?" the captain verified.

"Yes."

"You know Senator Henry?" he asked.

Melanie hesitated. "Yes."

"OK. Now, tell me what happened here."

Melanie and I interrupted each other in our haste to explain how we found him on the bed. Melanie said nothing about Jack McAllister being here with us, or about having shown the house to Henry earlier that morning.

"All right now, if you ladies will kindly stay right here, I need to have a look around." And the captain wandered off to explore the first floor.

"Wait a minute," Melanie called. "Where are you going? I just had those carpets steam cleaned."

The heels of the captain's boots were muddy.

Melanie ran after him with me right behind. "What are doing? What are you looking for?"

"I asked you ladies to wait out there in the hall."

"You have no right to take over this house. It's not like a crime has been committed here. There's no fire!"

The captain's face grew a deep red from the neck up, but quickly he calmed himself. When he spoke, his voice was quiet and calm. He must have taken classes in how to speak to hysterical females. "Ma'am, I'm a first responder. We've been trained in how to react to an emergency call. It's my job to take a look around, ensure the safety of my men and the rest of the emergency team. Make sure there's nothing hazardous here. It's the law. Ever hear of Homeland Security?"

Melanie was speechless. How had the day gone so wrong? Mere minutes ago she was on top of the world, on her way to earning a staggering commission.

"Hazardous?" I asked. "You mean like explosives?"

"Just let me do my job, ladies, please. I promise you I won't cart off the family silver." He attempted a joke.

Melanie and I strolled back to the front door which was standing wide open. "He's very condescending," she complained.

"Terrorists," I said. "He's been trained to look for terrorists. That'd be my bet.

"Something puzzles me, Mel. How did Henry get here? There was no car parked in the driveway. Did someone bring him? Then leave him here? After . . ."

An ambulance roared up the driveway and braked directly at the bottom of the porch steps, crushing a bush.

"Just look at what they're doing to the landscaping," Melanie cried with disapproval. "I'll have to replace that shrub."

"There was a pickup truck parked in the neighbor's driveway." I was thinking out loud. I looked out through the open door. "It's gone now." Where had I seen a truck like that recently?

Two paramedics hurried up the steps, bearing a gurney loaded with equipment. "Where's the patient?" one asked.

The captain appeared from the bedroom wing and escorted them up the stairs.

"You aren't going to tell them about Jack, are you?" I asked.

"Shush," she said, and shook her head.

"You're making a mistake."

"We'll see. Let's just let this play out. We don't know what happened to the senator. Could be a heart attack or a stroke. Natural causes."

"Sure, sure," I said doubtfully.

Within minutes, the EMTs were streaming back down the stairs, the firemen close behind.

The captain paused to speak to Melanie, perhaps felt she was owed an explanation. "This house is up for sale and you're the listing agent, right?"

He knew all that. Melanie nodded.

"We recognized Senator Henry but we verified his identify from his wallet anyway. Sorry to have to tell you but he's dead."

"Do you know how he died? Was it a heart attack?"

"We won't know that until the state medical examiner performs an autopsy and we get toxicology. We've called Wilmington PD. We're required to have a police report in a case like this. They're on their way. And the local M.E.'s coming. They'll arrange for transport to Chapel Hill. They'll even notify the next of kin."

Seeing Melanie's stricken face, the fire captain said, "Don't worry, ma'am. The police will handle everything. And we'll stay here with you until they arrive."

Then spotting the flash of sunlight off a glass windshield, he said, "Won't be necessary. Here they are now."

He strode out onto the porch, waved off the paramedics who were stowing their equipment in the rear of the ambulance, and gazed on as two police cruisers pulled up onto the grass.

Uh oh. The door to one of the cruisers was opening, and no, oh no, not him. I felt Melanie's breath near my ear. "It's him," I said.

She rested her hand on my shoulder. I reached up to clasp it. "Don't let him get to you," she said.

Don't let him get to me. Was that possible? We were like oil and water.

The firemen were ready to leave but waited as the captain took a moment to greet the man who had stepped out of the police cruiser. They shook hands and exchanged words.

Two uniformed officers and two plain clothes detectives entered the house. One of the detectives, heart-breakingly attractive, glared at me. Poison darts shot from his eyes to mine.

"Hi, Nick," I said in an off-hand manner. But the voice inside my head told me I was a fool if I thought he wasn't going to create a gigantic unpleasant scene about my being here.

Homicide Detective Nicholas Yost is my ex-husband. Ours had been a hot romance, a powerful bright candle that desire had ignited at both ends with such scorching intensity it had burned itself out – fast. Snuff. It was out. Over and done in just about a year.

"Ashley, what is it about you that draws you to every suspicious death in this town? The press is right about you. You are a magnet for murder."

I rebelled. "Murder? Who said anything about a murder? You've got a sixty-year-old man on the bed who probably died of natural causes. Maybe he had a stroke. Or a heart attack. Why don't you wait until the medical examiner does his job? You're the one who's the magnet."

I was tempted to say maggot but did not. Too petty even for me. I was pretty darn fed up with Nick and his sanctimonious attitude. It wasn't my fault that a senator had somehow entered Melanie's for-sale house, laid down on the bed, and proceeded to have some sort of medical problem. We'd already been informed that there would have to be an autopsy to determine cause of death. Why was Nick assuming a crime had been committed and that somehow I'd brought this distressful situation upon law enforcement and the tax payers?

The uniformed officers stood around, fascinated by the conflict between Nick and me. Abruptly, Nick started up the stairs, then turned back to Melanie and me. "You too stay right here. I'll talk to you later."

"Oh no, they are not," an angry but firm voice said from the open door. Jon. My hero. "I'm taking Ashley home. She's got two babies who need her."

"Yeah, I heard about the babies," Nick said, some of the flame in his fire dampened.

Jon went on, "Melanie is leaving too. You know where to find both of them when you get around to questioning them.

"And if you think that either one of them had anything to do with whatever . . . whatever went on here . . . then, as usual you are guilty of . . . well, the kindest thing I can say is lack of good judgment."

And with that, my darling, wonderful, brave husband slipped one arm around my waist and the other around Melanie's and propelled us out the door.

I turned for one final look at Nick. For just a second his expression had softened. I wondered if he was remembering the baby we had lost, the child who had not lived for more than three months after being conceived.

11

"Melanie, there is no way we are going to lie to the police," I hissed at her. "Tell her. Tell her, Walt. She must tell them the truth."

"I'm an officer of the court, Melanie. If there is something you have not been forthright about, now is your chance to set the record straight."

Attorney Walter Brice was thick around the middle, totally bald – in fact, I think he shaved his head - and pushing sixty. Taciturn by nature, and shrewd in his legal affairs, Walt had a soft spot for Melanie and me because of his friendship and admiration for our late father. Walt thought the world of Daddy, often referring to him as the best judge to ever preside over the New Hanover County superior court.

"Just tell the truth," Walt advised. "However, don't volunteer anything. Wait for the questions, then answer them succinctly but truthfully. No embellishments, please."

"The lieutenant will see you now," the clerk outside the lieutenant's office told us, opening the door to the office, and ushering us inside.

The big man who came lumbering out from behind his desk smiled broadly at Walt and reached forward to shake hands. "Walt Brice! How you doin', you old scallywag?"

After greetings, Walt introduced Melanie and me, and we found seats.

The lieutenant placed one large hip on the front edge of his desk, telegraphing that this was going to be an informal interview. To Melanie and me, he said, "Ladies, thank you for coming in. I'm Lieutenant Sol Edmunds. Because of the nature of this case, and also because Detective Yost has a personal connection to you, Mrs. Campbell, I've asked him to excuse himself from this interview. I will personally oversee these preliminary proceedings. That is, until we know the cause of Senator Henry's death. And I have no reason to believe that will be anything other than natural causes."

The last thing the lieutenant would want would be the homicide of a state senator in his jurisdiction. I realized he just wanted this thing to go away, same as we did.

"Nonetheless, his death is receiving a lot of media attention, as I'm sure you know by now."

Television new broadcasts around the state were reporting on the senator's untimely and inexplicable death. Questions were being raised about what the senator might have been doing inside an unoccupied, for-sale house. And some of the gossipy types of newscasters were speculating that he might have had a personal relationship with Melanie –

whom they referred to as Mrs. Cameron Jordan to further imply an impropriety.

"With all of the attention now focused on his office, the medical examiner is moving swiftly to arrive at cause of death. And the toxicology report will be processed as speedily as possible."

Melanie bestowed the lieutenant, and Walt, with one of her dazzling smiles, the kind that ordinarily causes men's hearts to falter. "Lieutenant, could you please get the press to call off the dogs? Tell them to lay off? They are ripping my reputation to shreds, hinting at all sorts of unseemly and inappropriate goings on."

She pressed the splayed fingers of her right hand over her heart. "I'm married to the state's most prominent television and motion picture producer. Imagine how embarrassing this is for my husband. And for me. I am about to be installed as the president of the North Carolina Association of Realtors. My reputation is impeccable, otherwise my fellow realtors would not have elected me to represent them."

Lieutenant Edmunds folded his arms across his chest, hearing her out. Melanie was more than he had bargained for. "I've heard of you by reputation, Mrs. Jordan."

"Ms. Wilkes. I'm known as Ms. Wilkes. And my sister is known as Ms. Wilkes. We are professional women."

"Of course," the lieutenant said. "And I know of your husband, Cameron Jordan, as well. And, as you say, so far as I know, your reputations are impeccable. But it's not only the press who are bringing pressure to bear, it's political organizations as well. And the governor's office, and members of the General Assembly."

Melanie stared up at him with flashing green eyes. "But put yourself in our shoes, Lieutenant. Can you imagine how destructive these rumors are to my husband's profession?" Melanie asked, managing to project justifiable outrage. "And for mine? Why that man chose to die in a house I have listed for sale has nothing to do with us."

"What do want to ask these ladies?" Walt asked in a friendly tone.

"Are you representing both of them?"

"I'm not aware that they need representing, Sol. I'm just here as a family friend. Their father . . . and I'm sure you remember Peter Wilkes . . ."

The lieutenant nodded. "Of course, we all thought the world of Judge Wilkes."

". . . was a good friend of mine. I'm here to guide his daughters through the process. Nothing more."

Even I began to relax. Walt had a way of making you believe there was nothing he couldn't handle and that everything was going to turn out all right.

The lieutenant's grip on his upper arms tightened perceptibly. Then he took a deep breath while lowering his arms and resting his hands on the desk top.

"Okay, ladies, just walk me through yesterday. Tell me about entering the house, and how and when you discovered Senator Henry. Who wants to start?"

"I will," I said. Still wanting to protect Melanie from Jack McAllister's wrath I thought that if I spilled the beans, she could always tell him it had been me who revealed his presence there. She would be off the hook.

And so without embellishments, as Walt had advised, I described driving out to Bradley Creek with Melanie, of meeting Jack McAllister there – at which point both Lieutenant Edmunds's and Walt's eyes widened – and then went on to describe entering the house.

Moving quickly for such a large man, Lieutenant Edmunds cornered his desk and settled heavily in his chair. "I think I need to record this," he said, reaching for a small tape recorder. "Any objections, Walt?"

"None whatsoever. My clients have nothing to hide."

"Clients?" Edmunds arched his eyebrows as if vaguely amused.

With the tape recorder running, I continued my tale of exploring the house with Melanie and Jack. Of how the three of us had remained together until Melanie's phone rang and Jack entered the master bedroom alone. Of how he had yelled for us to come at once.

"We saw that something was wrong with the senator," I said.

"Wait a minute. You recognized him right away? You knew who he was?" the lieutenant asked.

"Yes, we both know him. I met him Saturday night. He was a guest at Melanie's flotilla party."

"Let me understand." He turned to Melanie. "You socialized with Senator Henry?"

"No, I wouldn't characterize our association that way. It's a business relationship. I've met him a couple of time at realtors' conventions and political fundraisers. This was the first time I'd invited him to a party."

I interjected, "We called 9-1-1 as soon as we found him and saw that he was . . . having some sort of medical emergency. The firemen came and the paramedics. And then Nick . . . that is Detective Yost . . . came. You know the rest," I finished.

"No, actually, I don't," the lieutenant said firmly. "I don't know why McAllister did not remain, why he left."

I pressed my lips together. "You'll have to ask him that."

Walt intervened, "I think that is a question best addressed to Mr. McAllister."

"I intend to." Then the lieutenant focused his attention on Melanie. "Ms. Wilkes, do you have anything to add to your sister's statement? Do you agree this is way the events transpired?"

"Yes, my sister Ashley described finding Senator Henry exactly as it happened. But I do have something to add."

She gave Walt a warning glance. She wanted him prepared for what came next.

"As Ashley said, we both hardly know – knew Senator Henry. However, he is also a client. I showed him the house yesterday morning."

"You showed him the house?" the lieutenant asked slowly. "You took him into the house?"

Melanie nodded her assent.

"You'll have to speak up."

"Yes," she said then repeated loudly for the tape recorder, "yes."

"Tell me about that? How did the senator appear? Was he short of breath? Stressed? Did you notice anything out of the ordinary?"

"I didn't notice anything unusual. I met him there at the house at nine a.m. I showed him through the house. He had no trouble climbing the stairs. He seemed fine."

"And then what happened?"

"He admired the house but admitted it was out of his price range. I couldn't help wondering why he was wasting my time, if you must know. But in my business you see all kinds," Melanie answered.

"And did he leave with you?"

"He did. I saw him get into his car and drive away. I stayed behind to lock the front door."

"So the house was secure when you left?" Lieutenant Edmunds asked.

"I believed that it was secure, but when I was showing Jack and my sister around, I went to unlatch a sliding glass door only to discover that it was already unlatched."

"And you believe that is how Senator Henry entered the house again."

Melanie looked defenseless and I reached out to grasp her hand and comfort her.

"I don't know."

Walt said, "Ms. Wilkes wasn't there when the senator re-entered the house. She doesn't know how he gained access."

"One final question, Ms. Wilkes. Do you know why Mr. McAllister left the scene before the first responders arrived?"

Melanie compressed her lips and glanced up at the ceiling. "I don't know. Maybe he had an important meeting."

"Ed, if there is nothing else, I've got appointments, and these ladies have obligations as well."

Walt stood, terminating the interview. Melanie and I stood up as well.

Before departing, Walt said, "Ed, I trust that as soon as you have the autopsy report and the cause of death report, you will be good enough to share them with me before the press gets onto them. The late judge's daughters' reputations are on the line."

"If I can, Walt, I will. All depends on what the medical examiner finds. Thank you for coming in, ladies." And the lieutenant buzzed his clerk to show us out of the maze that was Wilmington's Police Department's headquarters.

But as we were leaving, the lieutenant said, "By the way, Ms. Wilkes, what kind of car was the senator driving when you met him at nine?"

Melanie paused to think. "A dark red Ford Explorer. I remember thinking that the senator was smart to be driving an American-made car."

Out on the sidewalk, Walt told us, "Do not talk to anyone unless I am there with you. As soon as we have the autopsy report we'll know what we are dealing with here. Until then, you both need to keep a low profile. If the lieutenant contacts you again – if anyone from law enforcement contacts you, and that includes Nick, Ashley, call me at once."

Melanie drove me home. As we drove, I gazed out of the car window, reviewing in my mind our statements to the lieutenant. "Everyone's putting up Christmas decorations," I said sadly. "Here this is supposed to be the happiest time of my life – I've got the man of my dreams and two precious, healthy babies – and it's their first Christmas, for pity sakes. But what am I involved in? The unexplained death of a politician I didn't even like!"

Melanie reached over to grasp my hand. "Don't be sad, little sis. We'll get through this and come out smelling like roses. We always do. I, for one, am not going to even think about Senator Henry and his untimely death. Just put it out of your mind. Like me."

"I'll try," I said.

We turned west on Nun and pulled into the second driveway on the right. My house. My lovingly restored 1860 Queen Anne Victorian house that had been built for a Quaker minister and his family before the Civil War. Crossing the front porch, I noticed again the plaque from the Wilmington Historical Foundation. "Reverend Israel Barton House," it read, and then the date, "1860."

As we climbed the front porch steps, Melanie called, "Cam's here. His van is out there on the street," and she pointed to a dark blue Lexus SUV parked at the curb under a low branch of a live oak tree.

The first greeting I got as I opened my front door was the fragrance of pine. I followed my nose and the sound of male voices back to the red library, the hub of our home. Sitting on matching leather sofas across from each other were our men.

"Oh, how adorable," Melanie said from behind me. "I've got to get a picture of this." And she dug in her shoulder bag for her camera.

"How did it go?" Cam asked.

"Don't ask," she replied. "It was dreadful. We'll talk about it later. Let's not spoil this moment."

I shared her pleasure in the moment. Jon held one baby on his lap; Cam held the other. Each was feeding a child from a bottle and the babies were sucking greedily. A breast pump had come into my life along with all of the other baby paraphernalia.

There was no missing the huge, fragrant Christmas tree that dominated one corner. It was strung with fairy lights but the other decorations remained unpacked in boxes strewn around the room.

"So that's what I smell!" I cried with delight. "Where did this come from? I didn't think we were decorating this year," I told Jon.

"You can thank your thoughtful brother-in-law," Jon said, and hoisted little Jonathan – or was it Peter? – onto his shoulder to burp.

"Cam? You brought us a tree?" I gave Cam a broad smile. What a nice guy? No wonder I love him so much.

Melanie was busily snapping pictures of the men caring for the babies.

"It's beautiful," I said. "You must have bought the biggest tree on the lot."

"It's about twelve feet," Cam said proudly.

I bent over him and gave him a kiss on the forehead. "No wonder Melanie adores you. I do too."

Cam gave Melanie a dreamy look. Then he looked down at little Peter – or was it Jonathan? "I want one of these," he told her.

And I thought Melanie was going to faint dead away.

12

According to tradition, the first weekend in December is reserved for the Olde Wilmington by Candlelight festival when historic homes are decorated in period style and put on tour. Ordinarily Jon and I would visit homes on both days even if, this year, it meant wheeling a double stroller. But Saturday was one of Dr. Amy Wood's infrequent days off. On Sundays she volunteered at the Pediatric Trauma Center at New Hanover Regional Hospital.

Saturday morning found us driving back out into Brunswick County to visit her historic house.

As we drove up the rutted, sandy lane and approached the house, all was quiet. I stepped down from the Escalade and paused a moment to enjoy the stillness, only some breezes in the longleaf pines stirring the tree tops.

"To think that my ancestors settled this land and lived here for generations. And I knew nothing about them. It's hard to believe," I told Jon.

"I can understand how this is hitting you emotionally. Melanie too. My roots are in Robeson County. I grew up hearing about the Campbell clan and how we emigrated from Scotland. We need to drive up there soon to visit Granny Campbell. She just about raised me, you know."

I moved closer to him and gave him a kiss. "And she did a mighty fine job of raising you. See how wonderfully you turned out." I gave him a squeeze. "It's peaceful out here."

"When the dogs aren't hunting foxes," he said.

"Here's a thought, Jon, let's give the boys another month to mature, then we'll take them to Granny Campbell's so she can see them."

"She'll fall in love with them. Good idea." He gave me a hug.

"No necking allowed on my property," Amy Wood called cheerfully from her front porch.

Amy isn't much older than I am but she has graduated from Duke medical school with honors, did her internship there, and is now set up in private practice. Her reputation as a pediatrician is sterling.

Amy is on the tall side – taller than I am at five-four but that isn't saying much. Most everyone is taller than I. Amy has auburn hair like Melanie and green eyes too. But Melanie gets her looks from Mama who was a Chastain, not a Wood, which leads me to believe this tendency toward red hair and green eyes runs in both sides of our family – from the Chastains and the Irish Hugheses. Amy wears her hair in a very short style, I guess because she is just too busy to blow dry long waves.

I'm a brunette with gray eyes and look a lot like my father, Peter Wilkes. I inherited his serious expression, his stubborn curly hair.

"Come on in. Let me show you around inside."

The house was Greek Revival in style, white paint over bricks that was peeling and had turned a dingy gray.

"Only the central section is original," Amy explained as she held the screen door wide for us to pass through. "The side and back wings are additions, added over time."

"Just let me get my camera," Jon said and returned to the car.

"Jon has state-of-the art architectural software that he uses to measure houses," I told Amy. "He takes pictures with a six millimeter camera, then when we get home, he'll feed the pictures into the computer and this special program will measure the rooms for us."

"I don't know what we'd do in medicine without the advanced technology," Amy said. I followed her into a small center hallway that ran the length of the house and Jon came in behind me carrying the camera.

Amy gave us a tour of the house and it was as I expected, very run down, plumbing and wiring out of date. But there was fine cabinetry everywhere. I made notes as we toured. Then Amy and I went out into the kitchen for iced tea while Jon took pictures of the house, inside and out.

We sat at the kitchen table. "Jon has filled me in about the deplorable practice of penned fox hunts," I told Amy. "I admire you for saving those foxes. How can these people call themselves sportsmen? There is nothing sporting about killing a trapped animal. Might as well shoot fish in a barrel."

"Foxes are such timid animals," Amy said. "They hide from people and aren't a threat to them. They actually help farmers control the rodent population. But Henry's fox pen is small compared to many in the state. There are about 150 fox pens in the state and the state Wildlife Commission looks favorably upon this practice. The only groups standing up to oppose this cowardly sport are the animal rights groups." Amy's face grew flushed with anger.

"But didn't you say that transporting wild animals is illegal?"

"It is, Ashley. A woman up in Pennsylvania tried to do a good deed by moving a deer from a populated area to a forested one. Only thing is she crossed state lines. And she was arrested. It is illegal."

"So why doesn't the Wildlife Commission enforce the law?" I was indignant.

Jon returned to the kitchen. "Where do you think the Wildlife Commission gets its revenue?" he asked. "From hunters. They've got a powerful lobby."

"Just think," Amy said, "when this house was built by Samuel Wood back in 1781, hunting was necessary to feed one's family. Today we have supermarkets on every corner. Deer are so tame, if you stand out by the side of the road at night they'll come up and eat out of your hand. Still they shoot them, cut off the antlers and leave the carcasses to rot. You tell me what is sporting about that."

"What has happened with Senator Henry's penned farm since he died?" I asked.

"The papers say it was you and your sister who found him, Ashley. That must have been hard for you. Still, the world, and in particular this part of it, is better off without him. The man was evil.

"His farm? All is quiet. No more foxes smuggled in from other states."

"But that is illegal, you said."

"Sure, but local law enforcement looks the other way. These are good old boys whose idea of a wild animal is a dead wild animal, or else in a zoo."

I just shook my head, speechless.

"Henry's farm is small as these fox farms go. One man owns a farm that pens 50 foxes. The foxes are bait, live bait, enclosed by fences. They have been caught in steel-jaw traps, injured, then crowded onto trucks, and driven into North Carolina to be sold to these blood sport operators. Finally, their fate is to get ripped apart by a pack of dogs. All so the owner can make a few measly bucks in field trial dog fees without working like the rest of us do."

"I'm so glad you saved those three little foxes the other day," I said sadly.

"Tell me, Ashley. Jon. You're the parents of infants. If you had just watched your dog rip a fox to shreds, would you then want that animal in your home, near your babies?

"Definitely not," Jon said. "I'd never trust a dog that had been trained to kill for blood sport."

"Of course you wouldn't. Well, at least that asshole Dewey Carter is gone. Excuse my foul language. Henry's not alive to pay Carter so he split. Mrs. Henry sure will not. I called her the next day and was surprised when she took my call. Supposedly, she was in mourning. I offered her good money for that property. She's very agreeable. She told me the whole idea struck her as distasteful."

"Distasteful? That's a mild word," Jon commented.

My mind wandered. My memory had just been jogged. The black pickup truck that was parked in the neighbor's driveway out at Bradley Creek? Wasn't it similar to the one Dewey Carter drove?

Amy was saying, "She and the senator didn't have much of a marriage. She traveled a lot. Guess she found him distasteful too." Amy laughed for the first time.

"That land was part of the Wood family acreage. It used to belong to my grandfather. But then granddad got a little senile and sly old Henry took advantage of him and got him to sell that tract of land for a pittance. Granddad is turning over in his grave to think how his land has been desecrated. Granddad was the local family physician, a kindly man, who treated his neighbors whether they could pay or not. And to think folks here actually voted Buddy Henry into office."

Jon said, "The state senate and house both have introduced bills prohibiting penned animal hunts. One got approval, but then died in committee. The committee is the state wildlife committee. We all need to call our state representatives and express our outrage."

"We'll call on Monday," I said.

"Good," Amy said. "We need more people like you and Jon."

"In all fairness, Amy, most people don't know this is going on. I didn't until I was here the other day and saw with my own eyes."

"You're right, Ashley. When people find out they'll be as

outraged as we are. Fox News did an exposé on the practice in Georgia and that sure started a movement to end this cowardly practice. Cowards, that's what they are."

"I had no idea. I'm glad you're getting your land back in the family," I said. My family, I thought.

"I'm going to clean up that hellhole, plant trees and shrubs over there and turn it into a wildlife sanctuary. I've even got a friend who's a vet and a couple of volunteers eager to work on this project with me."

"Good for you."

"Excellent idea," Jon said.

I took a deep breath and plunged in. "Amy, I have something else I'd like to discuss with you before we get back to your plans for restoring the house. I have reason to believe we are descended from the same ancestors, Samuel and Elizabeth Wood. According to a historian, they are my – and my sister's – ancestors too. Our g5 grandparents."

I had made notes of my Wood family tree and I read the list to Amy.

"You're right, we are related, Ashley. And that delights me. Imagine, discovering we are distant cousins. That's great. So you are descended from Margaret Wood. Well, I am descended from Margaret's brother Hastings Wood. Hastings' son was David – a name used often in this family – and David's son was Kinard. That was my grandfather. His son, my dad, was Kinard Wood Jr. My grandfather practiced medicine as I said, until he got too old to practice."

"And that's when Senator Henry cheated him?" Jon asked.

"Yes. I was away at med school. And Daddy died young.

An accident. Granddad left this house and land to me. You and your family should feel welcome to come here to visit and explore the grounds anytime."

"Amy?" I asked holding my breath. "Have you ever heard a rumor about a family treasure?"

"A family treasure!" she laughed. "That's a hoot. Yes, I've heard that talk. Nonsense is what it is. The Woods were always as poor as church mice. Treasure? Wouldn't I love that."

"It's probably just my imagination. I thought that when I was a kid my father said we had a treasure. But Melanie is older and she swears he said no such thing." I laughed nervously. Lying does not come easily to me. "Just a childish idea but I felt like I had to ask you anyway."

Amy just shook her head mildly. "I sure wish there had been some wealth in this family. Now who . . .?

A car had pulled up outside the kitchen windows. A county sheriff's car. A deputy got out of the driver's side. Another man – a very familiar man – got out on the passenger side.

Jon moved to the window. "Good Lord, how did he find us here?"

"Oh, no, not Nick!" I moaned. "I'm starting to feel like I'm being stalked."

Amy moved up beside me to stare out a window. "Who's Nick?"

"My ex," I groaned. "Nick Yost. A homicide detective with Wilmington PD. Guess he's here courtesy of your sheriff."

"I don't have to let them in if they don't have a warrant,"

Amy offered.

"No. Go ahead. Let them in. Let's see what this is about."

Amy went out onto the screened kitchen porch, they exchanged a few words, and she showed them into the kitchen.

Nick took one look at me and frowned. "I thought that was your car out there. How do you do it, Ashley? You show up at every crime scene."

"I wasn't aware that my cousin's house was a crime scene, Nick," I said smugly.

He looked from me to Amy. The sheriff's deputy introduced himself as Deputy Ernest Smalley. "Detective Yost has a few questions for you, Dr. Wood. So do I. Concerns the death of Senator Henry. Can you tell me where you were on the morning of Wednesday, December 1st?"

Amy crossed her arms over her chest. In a firm but controlled voice she responded, "I was in my office, seeing patients."

"Can anyone confirm that?" he asked.

"My staff and my patients," she replied as if she was speaking to a child.

"And what hours were you there? Seeing patients?"

"From eight a.m. until six p.m. I grabbed a sandwich at my desk at about noon. Never left the office until evening. Satisfied?"

"You mind if I call your office."

"Not at all, Deputy. Speak to anyone on my staff." Her tone was sweetly sarcastic. She gave him her office number.

Nick broke in, "The sheriff's office here had a complaint

about you. That you threatened the senator's life. And the investigation of his death is being handled by the Wilmington PD."

"From that jackass next door, Dewey Carter, no doubt," Amy said. "No, Detective, I did not threaten to kill the senator. Doesn't mean I'm not happy that he's gone. I am."

"Amy," Jon interrupted, "maybe you'd better not say any more."

Now Nick noticed Jon and grumbled a hello.

I said, "Wait a minute, Nick. Why is the PD investigating his death? Do you have autopsy results? Oooooh, you must. You asked her where she was on Wednesday morning. So you must have time of death. And for you to come all the way out here . . . his death must have been suspicious. Was he murdered?"

I knew I wouldn't get a direct answer from Nick and I didn't. "You know I can't discuss the details of a case with you. But where were you on Wednesday morning? And you too, Jon?"

Jon was angry. "I met with a prospective client at ten. I was with her until 11:30. Then squeezed in a work-out at the Y. And grabbed a quick lunch at Le Catalan. I got home about thirty minutes before Melanie picked up Ashley. All verifiable, Nick. Sorry to disappoint you."

Deputy Smalley looked from one of us to the other. What had he stumbled into?

I looked at him and smiled a fake smile. "Hasn't Nick bothered to tell you that we have history? We were once married. Now we're divorced. I'm married to Jon."

The deputy said nothing but gave Nick a searching look.

Turning to Nick I asked, "I thought Lieutenant Edmunds took you off this case because of your personal relationship with me. And Melanie."

"I'm still working the case, Ashley. How would I know that you would be here? Visiting your cousin?" He said 'cousin' as if he didn't believe me.

"Getting back to the senator's death," Smalley said. "Dr. Wood, you've got a record of feuding with Senator Henry about that farm over there." And he pointed out the window. "So now I've just got to ask you outright. Did you hire somebody to take out the senator?"

Amy stared at him in astonishment. Then she started to laugh. And laughed so hard she about doubled over.

There's no denying it: laughter is contagious. Jon and I were chuckling too. The law enforcement types did not see the humor in the question.

Amy composed herself and said emphatically, "No, Deputy Smalley, I did not hire anyone to 'take out,' as you say, the senator. How did he die? You haven't told us that yet. I do hope he was torn apart by foxes." This she said with perfect innocence.

"I can't discuss cause of death with you, ma'am. And what goes on at that farm next door is legal. Hunting regulations are enforced by the state's Wildlife Resources Commission. We've got an overpopulation of foxes and coyotes around here."

Amy's face flushed with anger. "If that is so, Deputy, why are foxes and coyotes being smuggled in from other states? If there are so many of them here, why are the operators of those penned fox farms willing to pay smugglers for a truckload of injured and sick wildlife?"

"Who said that was true? That's just a rumor," the Deputy said defensively.

Amy balled up her fists. "A rumor I have seen with my own eyes. I've seen those trucks rolling into that farm next door. I've seen their cargo being unloaded. I've even got pictures that I'm posting on the internet. I'm setting up a website to expose this evil cowardly practice. And I'm naming names."

"Ma'am, that simply ain't true. You've been listening to those bleeding heart animal rights nuts."

"Well, Henry's out of business now, Deputy. So if someone did kill him – if he did not die of natural causes and from the questions you've been asking, it's safe to assume he did not – then that person deserves a medal."

Nick broke in. "What about you, Ashley? Where were you on Wednesday morning at about 10:30?"

"Oh, that must be the time of death." I rolled my eyes heavenward. "Why would I have anything to do with his death? I was introduced to the man just once. I don't even know him."

"You did find him dead. You were in the house where he died. So I've got to ask the question. OK? Where were you?"

"At home with my babies. And they can't vouch for me because as advanced as they are in their development, at three months they aren't speaking yet."

13

On Sunday morning Jon and I lingered over coffee in the library. The boys were cooing and kicking in their play pen – "playing" as we liked to call it – and making happy baby noises. Our tranquility was shattered by the shrill screeching of our doorbell as someone twisted it frantically.

"We have got to replace that thing with something melodious," Jon said for the hundredth time.

"On our to-do list," I said. "Way at the bottom."

"Let's be sure to move it to the top."

I hurried to the door to find the frantic person – my sister Melanie – chomping at the bit. Behind her Cam regarded me stoically.

Melanie rushed inside. "Have you seen this?" she shouted, thrusting the morning paper in my face.

"No. We've been playing with the babies. We haven't gotten around to reading the paper yet. What's wrong?"

"Let's go inside and sit down," Cam said calmly. He

moved Melanie along to our library where Jon waited and babies gurgled.

"Aren't they precious?" Cam said, going over to the playpen to stare down at them.

"Just look at this," Melanie declared, holding the front page of the *Star-News* aloft for us to see.

The headline screamed: SENATOR HENRY'S OXY OVERDOSE.

I grabbed the newspaper out of her hands. "What's oxy?" I asked, trying to talk and scan the article at the same time.

"Oxy. Short for oxycodone. The most popular prescription meds on the black market. It's a pain pill. Makes you feel euphoric. On top of the world. Remember the time when I was attacked in my house out on Rabbit Run?"

Melanie was referring to an attack by an intruder who struck her on the back of the head, leaving her bleeding and unconscious, and suffering a concussion.

"Of course I remember. How could I forget?"

"Well, the doctor gave me a prescription for oxycodone. And it worked like magic. No pain. I can understand how people get addicted. I could feel myself relying on it too much. I threw the pills away."

"I didn't know that."

"I thought I told you."

"She told me," Cam said. "I was there when she flushed the pills down the toilet. She's such a brave girl." He gave her a hug.

Melanie broke free. She was incensed. "Somehow this investigative reporter found out that I once had a prescription for oxy. I don't know how he found out. That was what . . . two years ago? And now this reporter is insinuating that I am involved with Senator Henry's death."

"How? Just because you once had a prescription for oxycodone? You and how many other people?"

"It gets worse," Melanie said. "The oxy was mixed in with coffee. And the senator ingested it that way. According to his personal physician, the senator did not have a prescription for oxycodone. So someone drugged his coffee with a lethal dose of oxy. Remember when I was showing the house to you and Jack and there was a Starbucks coffee cup on the counter. I thought the cleaning service had left it there. I picked it up and threw it away."

"Oh, no!" I exclaimed, getting the full gravity of what she was saying. "The police found it. And your fingerprints are on it!"

"Exactly. And it gets worse. The chairman of the nominating committee called me first thing this morning. I'm out. They have kicked me out. They took a vote. I will not get to be president. She told me my reputation is in tatters and the NCAR cannot afford this bad exposure."

"Oh, Melanie." I rushed forward and put my arms around her. I knew how much this presidency meant to her. How hard she had worked for it.

"Can't we do something about this?" Jon said to Cam.

"We're working on it. But how do you deal with rumors and innuendo? Walt Brice is meeting us at police headquarters. We're going to try to sort this out."

"And we want you to go with us," Melanie said. "You saw

that coffee cup. You saw me pick it up. And you know I did not bring it into the house."

Attorney Walter Brice was waiting for us at the Police Department Headquarters on Bess Street. Then we were ushered into Lieutenant Sol Edmunds's office. He greeted us formally and did not offer his hand. Today, he was all business.

"Miss Wilkes, we've got a serious problem here. We've got the coffee cup that contained drugged coffee. And your fingerprints are on the cup."

Walt leaned back in his chair and tented his fingertips thoughtfully. "Tell me, Sol, how do you know the senator drank from that cup? How do you know he did not simply swallow a few pills on his own?"

The Lieutenant grimaced. "Technology, Walt. Traces of saliva on the cup's rim match the senator's DNA. The autopsy showed the ingested coffee with grains of oxy. And a bit of coffee in the bottom of the cup showed the same.

"Since this is a state senator's death, we asked the state bureau for help. They sped up testing in their labs."

"Are the senator's prints on the cup? What about the person at Starbucks who served the coffee? Any other prints?" Walt asked.

"No other prints," Edmunds said.

"What?" Walt roared.

Melanie, Cam and I were an enthralled audience to this exchange.

Lieutenant Edmunds clasped his hands on his desk top and leaned forward toward Melanie. "Miss Wilkes, we've spoken to Jack McAllister. He has an alibi for the time of death. He was just leaving Charlotte at 10:30 on the morning of December 1st. His cell phone's GPS and his car's GPS confirm his statement."

Melanie simply stared at him, seemingly flummoxed at all that was happening. Was she going to be charged with murder?

"Where were you at 10:30 on December 1st?"

Melanie frowned but did not answer.

"Melanie, you need to answer him," Walt advised.

"Oh, all right. It's true that I met Senator Henry there at the house at nine. But we left the house at about 9:30. He couldn't afford it. Why he wasted my time, I don't know. And I remember locking the house as we left. But later when I showed the house to Jack and my sister, one of the sliding glass doors was unlocked.

"I think the senator was meeting someone there. I think he used me to get into the house and to have a private place to meet someone secretly."

I jumped in. "I saw a black pickup truck parked in a neighbor's driveway. The senator's foreman Dewey Carter drives a truck just like it. Maybe he's the one who was meeting Senator Henry at Bradley Creek."

The Lieutenant said, "I'll look into it. But if they work together at Henry's property, why would they need to meet clandestinely at Bradley Creek?"

I was frustrated. Did I have to do all the thinking? "I don't know. Maybe they were working on something else. And they didn't want to be seen together. All I know is there was a truck nearby that day that looked like Carter's."

Edmunds made a note.

I went on, "And I overheard a quarrel between the senator and Wren Redfield. A violent quarrel. They almost came to blows."

"When was this?"

"On Saturday evening, at Melanie's flotilla party."

The Lieutenant got a thoughtful look on his face. "But Redfield died that night. Are you suggesting he came back from the dead to kill off the senator?"

"Sol," Walt said warningly.

"Sarcasm isn't necessary," Cam interjected.

Now I was mad. "Of course I'm not suggesting that. I'm simply pointing out that Senator Henry had enemies. So while you are focusing on my sister, you are not focusing on his enemies."

"I'm looking at all the possibilities."

He directed his attention back to Melanie. "You still haven't answered my question, Miss Wilkes. Where were you at 10:30 that morning?"

"Well, I don't want this to get out. It's something I don't talk about. Everyone thinks I have such beautiful skin – you know, naturally."

Walt and Edmunds just stared at her. What was she talking about?

"If you insist on knowing, I was at my dermatologist's, having a chemical peel. My little secret." She twisted her mouth.

The lieutenant sat back, silenced. "I suppose you can prove that."

"Of course," Melanie replied.

He gave a little smile, and looked like he was about to shake his head and mutter: Women!

Then he said, "Jack McAllister also reports that you saw the coffee cup, was angry that the cleaning service had left it behind, and picked it up to throw it in the trash basket."

"I was there," I exclaimed. "I saw that happen too. Melanie did not bring that coffee cup into the house. And if you presume she brought it there earlier, and filled it with poison to kill Senator Henry – a ridiculous notion – why would she leave it there to be discovered?"

The lieutenant smiled patiently. "That is what I am getting at. There was only one set of fingerprints on that cup. Yours, Miss Wilkes. When there should have been at least three: yours, the senator's, and the employee at Starbucks who poured the coffee.

"That is why I say, Miss Wilkes, we have got a problem. Who is trying to set you up? Help me figure that out and we've got our killer."

Jon insisted we needed a break from the stress of the murder and mayhem that had infiltrated our lives once again. We tucked the babies into their stroller and wheeled them up Third to Market Street and the Burgwin-Wright house.

"This is a wonderful idea," I told Jon as we got in line to tour the house. I gave him a little hug. "You're so smart. You know what I need before I do."

The two-story white frame house with double porches was decorated in the holiday spirit of 1770. When our turn came, we lifted the stroller and carried the babies up onto the front porch. Of course, they caused quite a stir, garnering as many accolades as the house itself.

The Burgwin-Wright house was built in 1770 by John Burgwin, at one time treasurer for the colony of Carolina, upon the site of the old town jail. A tunnel led from the jail to the riverfront and was the source of many myths. One such legend was that when Lord Cornwallis departed Wilmington for Virginia, he left patriots behind, locked in the dungeon beneath the house. The story goes that those men were able to escape starvation and death by making their way through the tunnel to the riverfront.

As Jon and I entered the house, I said, "If it's true that an ancestor of mine was held prisoner here, well, it makes me feel a strong connection to this house and to that time in our history."

"I'm sure it makes you feel proud," my husband said.

"Yes," I murmured.

Then we got caught up in the tour and I gazed again at the beautiful antique furniture, the rose damasks, the pink and white china. "Oh," I exclaimed, "there it is. My favorite." And I stared up at the beautiful Waterford crystal chandelier.

As we left the house, I told Jon, "That was just what I needed. I feel grounded again."

"The boys are asleep. What do you say we stop by LeCatalan for a bowl of hot soup."

"You are so full of good ideas today," I said, slipping my arm through his. "Any thoughts about how we might spend the rest of the evening?"

He grinned at me. "As you say, I'm just full of good ideas."

14

"I don't understand why you have to attend Wren Redfield's memorial service," Jon complained as he watched me dress. "It's not like you knew him. You only met him the night he died."

"I was the one who discovered him on the stairs," I said. "No, I take that back. That blonde pony-tailed so-called babysitter was the first one to find him." I was still sore about that nineteen-year-old trying to put the make on my man.

"Look, Jon, it's like this. Melanie has to put in an appearance. And she's a wreck because of the accusations the news media are making. If she doesn't go, people will think she's hiding something, that there must be some truth to the allegations."

"Why can't Cam go with her?"

"He would if he were in town but he's up in Raleigh with a delegation of movie people. They're meeting with some members of the General Assembly. Jon, she's not nearly as confident as she lets on. She needs me."

My gorgeous husband pulled me down onto his lap. "The kids need you. I need you. I need you very much. Right now." He put his hands on me in a very familiar way. His touch took my breath away.

I jumped up. "Hold that thought. I'll only be gone a short while. We aren't going to the church service. Just to the reception to pay our respects. Southport is a short haul. Melanie says we'll only stay long enough to be seen. Now I've got to finish dressing."

A devilish smile played on his lips. "Must you?"

I almost forgot my promise to Melanie. What would I rather do this afternoon? Attend the memorial reception for a man I barely knew? Or loll around in bed with my sexy husband? What a loaded question.

"Two hours. Just two hours. Then we'll pick up right here," I promised.

The Redfield's house overlooked the marina that they were expanding on a very grand scale. Melanie filled me on the expansion on our drive down. "Wren inherited a small marina that catered to locals, fishing boats for hire, motor boats. He had the idea to expand the docking facility to accommodate large yachts. You know, this area is really starting to attract a lot of wealthy yachters from all over. Then he'd use the land he owned - and there's just acres and acres of forested, undeveloped property in that family – to build restaurants, gift shops, maybe some high-rise condos.

"They're right across the Waterway from Bald Head Island and everyone knows how successfully the development of Bald Head turned out."

"What'll happen now that he's gone?" I asked.

"That'll be up to Regina." She turned to me.

"Watch the road," I shouted.

"Sorry," she muttered. Then eyes front, she went on, "You know, I've been thinking a lot about our conversation with Lieutenant Edmunds yesterday. Who *is* trying to set me up? Who benefits the most from the suspicion on me right now?"

"So who does?"

"I've always aroused jealousy in others. Particularly women. Ever since high school and my cheer leading days. And then on the pageant circuit. But right now, the person who benefits directly from my defeat is Regina Redfield.

"Regina has always been very complex. Driven and competitive. I think she's behind these ridiculous rumors about me. Setting out to ruin my reputation."

"But what good would it do her to ruin your reputation?"

"She already has. The nominating committee voted to rescind my presidency. They gave it to Regina who is next in line. So yes, she did stand to gain by having me removed."

"But why, Melanie? What would her motive be?"

Dark green trees flew back outside the Cadillac's tinted windows.

"You don't know anything about the real estate world, baby sister. And the politics surrounding it. The president of the NCAR wields a lot of power. Doors are opened to her. She has the ear of the decision makers in this state. It's a very influential position. And now Regina is getting that position, not me. And I've earned it."

She banged her fist against the steering wheel.

"But all she had to do was wait one year and the presidency would be hers," I offered.

"True," Melanie said thoughtfully. "There must be some reason, something that is immediate, to make her ruin me so she can take over the presidency now."

"But is it really that important? Isn't that office more of an honorary sort of position?"

She gave me a sharp glance. "Not at all. As I said, doors are open to the president. Doors that remain shut to your ordinary broker. Powerful people in state government become accessible. The governor. General Assembly members. Corporate leaders.

"If you're crooked – and you know I'm not – a realtor could parlay that position into maybe getting some favors, feathering her own nest."

"Like what?" I asked.

We pulled into the long white gravel driveway that led to Regina's waterfront home.

"Probably a lot that has never occurred to me. But just off the top of my head, reversing zoning restrictions, start-up incentives from state government. That sort of thing."

"And you think Regina needs the position because she wants a favor from someone in a high place?"

"That has occurred to me."

Melanie parked her silver Cadillac in an open slot in an expansive parking area at the rear of Regina's house.

"I had to come to this reception to prove I'm not in hiding. I'll keep my chin up and look everyone straight in the eye. Defy them to think the worst. But I'm also here to keep a sharp watch over Regina. You know the saying: keep your friends close but your enemies closer."

The Redfield house was historic, a sprawling white clapboard house that had been built by one of Wren's ancestors in the nineteenth century, and then restored by Regina when she married Wren. On the inland side, acres and acres of forested land. And on the water side, the marina that was undergoing dredging and expansion.

About fifty people milled around, talking to each other, serving themselves from a buffet table in the dining room. I recognized many of Melanie's realtor friends.

"Hi, Ashley," someone said, as Melanie was drawn into a conversation with two men.

I turned to find a familiar face, but for a second could not place him because we'd only met once. Roger Craighead. "Roger," I said. "Hello." A little surprised to see him here. "You knew Wren?"

He smiled pleasantly. "Regina is my aunt. She was a Craighead before she married Wren. My father's sister."

"Oh," I said. "Then Wren was your uncle. By marriage. I'm sorry for your loss."

"And I've been hearing how you and Melanie found Senator Henry in that vacant house. That must have been a shock." He nibbled from a buffet plate in his hand.

"Yes, quite a shock."

Regina approached, making the rounds, greeting her guests. She was dressed all in black, a single strand of matched pearls. "You must be talking about finding Senator Henry."

Melanie excused herself from the men to join us. She gave Regina a hug and kissed the air at her cheek. I remembered her promise to keep her enemies close. "Regina, sweetie, I am so sorry for your loss."

Regina pulled away but took Melanie's hand. "And I'm so sorry for the way the nominating committee has been treating you. I want you to know I had nothing to do with them rescinding your presidency and moving me forward."

"Of course you didn't, sugar. That wouldn't be like you. But I'm trying to put myself in their places. If I were on the nominating committee, I'd do the same. The publicity about me has been dreadful. Groundless but dreadful."

Roger Craighead looked from one of them to the other, politely following the conversation.

Melanie got syrupy sweet. "Regina, you can't imagine how dreadful I feel that it was my stairs that Wren fell on."

"You mustn't blame yourself, Melanie. It was an accident. And Wren had too much to drink. I don't want to hear another word along those lines. No one's to blame. Accidents happen."

I spotted Amy Wood across the room and tossed her a wave. A waiter came by with a tray of sodas and wine. I selected a glass of soda. Oh, I couldn't wait to get back to wine drinking.

Melanie helped herself to a glass of white wine. "Regina, you'll make a fabulous president. And I want you to know if there is any way I can help you, I'll be more than glad to. You've got some catching up to do and I can help fill you in."

"Thanks, Melanie. And I want you to know that any committee you want to chair is yours."

"I just can't believe that we've lost Wren," Melanie said, seemingly heart felt. "And Senator Henry too. What is going on?"

"You're not the only one who'll miss Buddy Henry. The whole state will miss him."

But not the foxes I thought to myself as I sipped soda and watched Melanie perform and do a number on Regina.

"Buddy was so sensitive to the needs of his constituents. He was helping Wren and me with a big project. Our plans were to open a Las Vegas style casino here at the marina. None of that video stuff. This would be first class, like Vegas, with big name entertainers and free food. Buddy was going to introduce the bill in the General Assembly. We'd be private, members only. Closely supervised. It would have been such a boon for our marina. The Native Americans are allowed to have gambling casinos, why not us?"

Melanie looked startled but caught herself. I tried for a blank expression. "What a darling idea. I love it. Cam and I would join. What fun!"

"It would have been. We were going to let in only the best people," Regina said. "But now with the senator gone, well, I just hope I can find another sponsor."

"So you are proceeding with the expansion plans for the marina?" I asked.

"Certainly. They're much too far along to cancel now."

"Melanie, we'd better go. I've got to get back to my babies." I gave Regina a hug and shook hands with Roger. "Regina, would it be all right if Melanie showed me around your beautiful home before we left. You might have heard that I restore old houses like this. I like what you've done here."

"I decorated it myself," Regina said proudly. "Sure, go ahead. Melanie knows her way around. Show her the loft. The view from up there is spectacular."

"Be glad to."

We started for the stairs and the big open loft. "Now what . . .?" she started to say.

"Ashley! Hi!" Amy Wood intercepted us. "This must be Melanie. I'm a distant cousin, Melanie."

Melanie smiled and said hello.

"I didn't know you knew Wren and Regina," I said.

"The Redfields, the Craigheads, the Woods, we're all old Brunswick County families," Amy said. "Related too, but it's very complicated. Roger Craighead called and asked if he could come out and poke around the farm with a metal detector. He's a big enthusiast of the Revolutionary War and collects military artifacts." She sipped her Coke. "I told him I didn't think he'd find anything but he was welcome."

Oh, dear. Amy did not know about the hidden gold. But I did. And Roger did.

Amy added, "Just between us, I'll feel safer having him around the property. Someone's been trespassing. I find little signs that someone's been there. I think that hateful Dewey Carter is skulking around my house at night, trying to scare me."

"Have you called the sheriff?" I asked.

"Yes, but you can imagine how they responded."

"I'm sorry, Amy. Maybe you ought to stay in town for a while."

"I've considered that. But I hate to have some coward run me out of my own home."

Melanie said, "We're just about to leave, Amy, but I hope to see you again soon."

"Me too, Melanie," Amy said. "Before you go, I've got a bit of news to share. No secret. It will be all over the papers in the morning. Working at the medical center as I do, I'm in the loop. Anyway, the medical examiner finally got around to doing an analysis of Wren's blood. It wasn't a high priority like the senator's lab results. Wren's blood alcohol content was high as expected. Everyone said he had been drinking before he fell down the stairs. But here's the kicker. There was also a high level of OxyContin – that's a brand name for oxycodone – in his blood. That would help explain why he lost his balance. Oxy and alcohol. A lethal combination. We're seeing a lot of oxy ODs in the ER now that the drug is being pushed by every small-time drug dealer."

Melanie and I exchanged an alarmed look but tried to keep our expressions neutral.

"How interesting," I said. "Does Regina know?" I spotted Regina chatting with some well-wishers.

Amy shook her head negatively. "I don't know. But she will soon."

Melanie was dragging me away. "You'll have to come to my Christmas party, Amy. I'll call you."

Up in the loft we stood at the railing and gazed down into Regina's large living room. An expanse of windows looked out over the harbor where a stiff wind ruffled the water. Across the bay the Old Baldy lighthouse poked up into the sky.

In hushed tones I recounted the quarrel I'd overhead between Wren Redfield and Senator Buddy Henry on the night of Melanie's flotilla party. "Regina is lying. Buddy Henry told Wren very firmly that he was not going to introduce a bill for him. At the time I had no idea what they were talking about. But now we know Wren wanted him to sponsor a bill that would allow live casino gambling. Henry was adamant. He told Wren his constituents would kick him out of office. And you know with the ban on video sweepstakes passing the General Assembly and some people feeling strongly that even Lotto is a sin, Henry was right. He would have been kicked out. So why is Regina telling this story?"

"To make people think that she and Henry were friends? I'll tell you something, Ashley, you know Regina's perfect little nose? Well, she had a nose job in the spring. And dollars to donuts she got a prescription for oxy."

"Where's her bathroom? Let's take a look."

Melanie beamed. "How'd I get so lucky to have a sister like you? Come on, I know just where the master suite is located."

After confirming that Regina was not looking our way, we moved from the railing toward a hallway that ran to the front of the house. I rushed down the hall. "Slow down," Melanie hissed. "You look suspicious."

"No I don't," I argued. "I look like I have an urgent need for a powder room."

Melanie opened the door to a spacious bedroom that was done up in pale blue and white. An open door led into the bathroom. We hurried inside.

"Lock the door," I whispered. Melanie did.

Then I turned on the sink faucet. "This is no time to wash your hands," Melanie complained.

I gave her an exasperated look. "If Regina comes into the bedroom, she'll think someone is really using the bathroom. Not searching it."

Already Melanie was opening cabinet doors. "There!" she cried. She had opened a shallow wall cabinet and right on the middle shelf was a prescription bottle. The prescription was made out to Regina Redfield for OxyContin. Melanie stretched out her hand to pick up the bottle.

"Wait!" I hissed. I unrolled some toilet paper and handed her a tissue. "Use that."

Lifting the bottle out with the tissue, she shook it. "Empty." She dropped it into her purse.

We almost scurried down the stairs in our haste to leave. Passing Regina with some guests, Melanie blew her a kiss. "Bye, sugar. Now you take me up on my offer to help you with the NCAR, ya hear."

"Your house is gorgeous," I called over my shoulder.

Then we beat a hasty retreat to Melanie's Cadillac. As we drove out, I looked back to see Regina standing inside the glass storm door, a puzzled expression on her face.

15

The week flew by. Melanie and I took Regina's empty prescription bottle for oxycodone and our suspicions to Lieutenant Edmunds. Technically, it was Walt Brice who handed over the bottle, saying it had found its way into his possession but that attorney-client privilege prevented him from naming the source. A shallow lie that anyone could see through. Particularly as Melanie and I were present – a coincidence, professed Walt, as I was there to tell the Lieutenant the details of the quarrel I'd overheard between the two deceased men. One dying suspiciously of an oxy overdose, the other where oxy was a contributing factor to the fall.

The Lieutenant kept his own counsel, merely telling us he would look into the matter. I felt sure he was going to look closely at Regina Redfield who had everything to gain by the death of her husband and the senator.

From her husband she would inherit the Redfield marina, the lands, and his wealth. With Senator Henry out of the way, she could use the NCAR presidency she had stolen from

Melanie to find a sponsor for her bill, and would not have the powerful and influential Buddy Henry opposing her in the General Assembly.

In my book she was guilty. But the police do not confide in me about how they conduct their cases. From the grapevine I learned that no one had seen Regina since the afternoon of Wren's funeral reception. Melanie had tried calling her and left messages. Regina never did return her calls or respond to her offer of help in preparing for the presidency position. But let's face it, perhaps even Regina did not have that much gall.

Melanie was in a dither about her Christmas party plans for Saturday evening. Two hundred guests had been invited, and Melanie's good friend from high school, Elaine McDuff, was available to cater the party.

"You know, Mel, as soon as the police charge Regina with murder, the nominating committee will be groveling at your feet for you to come back and save them."

"I've thought the same thing," Melanie confessed. "I sure wish the police would hurry up with their investigation. Wonder if they checked *her* alibi for the morning the senator was murdered."

We were talking on the phone as we did each day. The restoration business is slow around the holidays as is the real estate business. Jon and I were enjoying a lot of fun family time watching the boys grow. When he had a free moment, Jon worked on the computer program that was converting his photos of Amy Wood's house into precise architectural drawings. Once the holidays were over, we'd resume work with her on our ancestors' house.

My phone line clicked. "I've got another call. Hold on, Mel."

The caller was Walt Brice. "Ashley, turn on your TV. The police chief is holding a press conference about Buddy Henry's homicide. I'll call Melanie."

"She's on the phone with me now. I'll tell her." I clicked back to Mel and repeated Walt's message. Then I headed for the library and the TV there, alerting Jon on the way.

The chief was standing behind a clutch of microphones outside headquarters. On the scene local news reporters stretched out their mikes toward him too.

Unfortunately we had missed his opening statements but were tuned in to the question and answer period. One reporter asked, "Sir, you said there was a warrant out for Regina Redfield. Does that mean you are charging her with murder?"

The chief was very much in charge and handled the media skillfully. "We are not charging Mrs. Redfield at this time. She is merely wanted for questioning."

"Would you call her a 'person of interest' in your investigation?" another reporter shouted.

"That would be fair to say."

"What makes her a person of interest, Chief?"

"Forensic evidence. That's all I can say except that it's very important that we find Mrs. Redfield and talk to her."

"Find her? What are you saying, Chief? Is Mrs. Redfield missing?"

"We haven't been able to locate her. Her staff and colleagues do not know where she is." He lifted his chin higher and looked directly into the cameras. "So if anyone has information about the whereabouts of Regina Redfield, please call the number that appears on your screen."

And a telephone number crawled across the bottom of the TV screen.

Jon came in and moved up close behind me, viewing the screen over my shoulder. "What's happening?"

"They're looking for Regina Redfield. She's missing."

A reporter called out, "Does this mean that Melanie Wilkes is no longer a suspect in the senator's death?"

The Chief said, "Ms. Wilkes has a verified alibi for the time of the senator's death. She is not now, nor has she ever been, a suspect."

I was holding the phone to my ear, still on the line with Melanie. "Did you hear that, Mel? You're in the clear."

Over the phone she let out a whoop of joy. Then I heard Cam say something to her. "Ashley, call me later. We've got a little celebrating to do here."

I laughed. "Sure, sis. Later." And I clicked off. I felt like doing a little celebrating of my own. And Jon is always up for celebrating.

On Saturday morning, our clan piled into our vehicles and headed out to the airport to pick up Scarlett and Ray. What a merry bunch we were, hugging and kissing, and loading our cars with their luggage. We drove them out to Wrightsville Beach to their beach cottage *Bella Aqua*. Aunt Ruby and Binkie were going to stay with them at Wrightsville through the holidays. On Monday morning, Cam and Jon were taking Ray on an excursion down College Road to buy a car that he'd leave in the garage under their house. Until then, we were happy to chauffeur them around.

By six o'clock that night, Regina had still not surfaced, and the news media was all atwitter. Her car was not missing but parked at her home, one resourceful journalist had determined. Had she taken a cab to the airport, he wondered aloud on a local news show. A spokesperson for Wilmington PD confirmed that the investigators had checked airline records and no one named Regina Redfield had departed Wilmington by air transit.

But something very interesting had turned up at the airport, specifically in the long-term parking lot. Buddy Henry's Ford Explorer!

"That clears up a mystery for me and it should clear it up for the police as well," I told Jon when the news show broke for commercials. "And that is, how did Buddy Henry get to the house at Bradley Creek. There was a black pickup truck in a neighbor's driveway and I suspected Dewey Carter drove the senator out there. But why?"

"Yes," Jon said. "Why there? Henry and Carter could have met anywhere in Brunswick County. Why would they have to sneak around at Melanie's listing house? I never did like that theory of the crime."

"It was a weak theory. My money is on Regina Redfield. She had some kind of hold over the senator. She lured him into the house."

"But only Henry could have unlatched the sliding glass door," Jon pointed out. He wagged his eyebrows. "So perhaps he was the one doing the luring."

"But Wren had just died," I reasoned.

"OK, so maybe the motivation wasn't sex. Maybe it was money."

"Here's something else, too, Jon. Wren Redfield fell or was pushed down the stairs. And remember at the Airlie light show, Melanie was sure someone had pushed her from behind, pushed her toward the lagoon. Maybe Regina Redfield was trying to get Melanie out of the picture as early as that. If Melanie had a serious 'accident' and was injured, she would be unable to assume the NCAR presidency."

"Good point. That's some . . ."

The journalist returned to the screen to say that sources had revealed Wren Redfield was addicted to oxycodone. A couple of years earlier, Redfield had been involved in a head-on collision with a telephone pole outside of Southport. Redfield had been drinking and driving too fast. He had sustained head injuries which caused severe headaches. The source, an unnamed associate of Redfield's, reported that Redfield had become dependent on oxycodone. When he could no longer obtain a prescription for the meds, he bought them from black market dealers.

"I wonder if Regina was sharing," I mused. "That would explain why her prescription bottle was empty."

"Or maybe it was empty because she used her pills to spike Senator Henry's coffee." Jon snapped off the evening news. "OK, enough about the Redfields and our current crime wave for one night. I want to see you in that new strapless evening gown." He nuzzled my neck and caressed me in intimate places. "I've gotta tell you, babe, you can sure fill out a strapless gown. I'll be the envy of every man at that party."

"Then unhand me, Sir, and I'll go get dressed. I think I have time for a bubble bath if our little darlings continue their nap."

Jon grinned wickedly. "Let me help."

The field beyond Melanie and Cam's home was crowded with cars and again Melanie had a valet parking the guests' vehicles. From the house came the voices of a chorus singing popular Christmas tunes. Melanie's Cadillac was parked in the circular drive and we had been saved a spot right behind it outside the front doors. Again Cam was watching for us and emerged to help Jon unload the babies and their paraphernalia. But first he kissed me. "Merry Christmas, Ashley." And gave Jon a big hug. "You guys look great. The nursery is all set up and ready for these little buggers. And this time, Melanie's got a professional nanny up there. Here, let me get that for you, Jon."

The men and the babies led the way and I followed into the lodge that looked so much like Biltmore at Christmas. There were green swags and garlands and gilded Christmas trees that reached the high ceiling. Lights glittered everywhere. It was like a fairyland.

A maid took my wrap as Melanie rushed out to greet me. She was flushed with happiness and looked beautiful in a sparkling white evening gown. My gown was red. We posed for the photographer *Wrightsville Beach Magazine* had sent to cover the party. Then she steered me off to the side and just about gushed, "Oh, shug, they're all here. The entire nominating committee. Perhaps 'groveling' is not the right word, but they surely do want me back. The chairman said she never stopped believing in me and knew that the allegations were nothing more than media hype, but she had no choice. She was forced by NCAR's high standards for their officers and just had to replace me. Now the spotlight is on Regina and it is not a flattering spotlight at all. Everyone is expecting her to be charged with murder. You heard the Chief say they had forensic evidence connecting her to Senator Henry's death."

"So tell me, what did you say? Did you accept?" I asked excitedly.

"I accepted, naturally. This is what I have worked for all of my career. I'll be inauguarated as originally planned. I'll be the new president. I just want to give out a cheer and jump in the air."

"Me too." I gave her a hug. "I'm so happy for you, big sis. You deserve good things."

At midnight, Melanie and I stood with our arms around each other in the doorway to the drawing room. "They love her," I said.

"Yes, they are enthralled," Melanie agreed.

"She is dazzlingly beautiful," I said.

"She looks more like Mama than I do," Melanie said.

"Yes," I said with an ache in my heart. "When Mama was young. Before that dreadful disease took her away from us."

"I know, shug. I know. Wouldn't she be happy that we are united with Scarlett?" Scarlett was our mother's love child.

And now Scarlett stood in the center of Melanie's drawing room, singing her way into everyone's heart. It was true the guests loved her. She wore an emerald green satin gown that made her green eyes sparkle. Ray accompanied her on the baby grand piano as she sang the best of Cole Porter: "What Is This Thing Called Love?"; "You Do Something to Me"; "All Through the Night".

After resounding applause, she led the guests in a sing-along of popular Christmas tunes and traditional carols.

I gave Melanie a kiss. "Wonderful party, Mel. You've outdone yourself." And then Cam joined her and they were surrounded by their guests, bidding them good night. Everyone calling "Merry Christmas" as they collected coats and headed out into the night.

And then it was just family.

"We'll never top this," Jon said, hugging me.

"Who would want to," I said.

He handed me the car keys. "Why don't you go on out and warm up the car. Cam and I will collect the babies. Aunt Ruby and Binkie, and Scarlett and Ray are up there now with them. I sent the nanny home."

"I'll walk out with Ashley," Melanie told Cam. "Then I'll run them over to Wrightsville. Tell them to take their time. I'll get the car heater going and meet them out front."

Melanie and I grabbed our coats and headed out into the night. I clicked my car door open and threw my purse inside. Then I turned to say goodnight to my sister. Out in her driveway, under a starry sky, we gave each other a rocking hug.

"I love you, Mel," I said. "Who would have thought that our lives would turn out so good? We've got so much to be thankful for this Christmas. I've got Jon and our babies. You've got Cam. Who is a good influence on you, by the way."

She giggled. "I *have* led a wicked life, haven't I? You know, little sis, at first I resented her but now I love having Scarlett in our family. Ray too. And Binkie and Aunt Ruby, of course. What would we do without them? We are blessed, Ashley. Blessed. Think you can meet me at the eleven o'clock service in the morning? Actually, it's already morning. Almost one."

I started across the driveway to the Escalade. "Sounds good. See you at church tomorrow."

I had turned as I spoke to her and was walking backward. And that is when I bumped into Santa Claus!

16

There in front of me stood a man in a Santa suit, complete with beard and glasses, and red hat. The glasses looked vaguely familiar. Had Melanie hired a Santa to entertain at the party? And was he late? Very, very late?

Melanie had moved up close to me. "Who are you? What are you doing here?"

She held up the car remote control with her thumb poised over it. I knew what she was about to do: sound the horn.

But Santa spoke mildly. "I think I'm lost. I'm supposed to be at a party but I think I turned up the wrong road."

Melanie relaxed. So did I. Just what he was waiting for. Quickly he reached out with his left hand and grabbed the remote from her. "I'll take that." In his right hand, he held a gun that he'd been hiding in his bulky costume.

He pointed the gun directly at us. "Get in," he ordered as he popped the trunk.

"I can't," Melanie argued. "I'll scream."

"You do and I'll shoot her." He grabbed me and pressed the gun to my temple.

"Don't shoot. Don't shoot. We'll do as you say."

She crossed to her car and stared down into the open trunk. "Please don't make me get in there. I've got claustrophobia. Just take the car. I'll give you a few minutes to get away. I don't want any trouble."

"In the trunk, I said!" He was dragging me toward the open trunk. Then he was pushing me inside. "Get in!" he yelled at Melanie.

There was scarcely room enough in the trunk for two people but Melanie squeezed inside, crying and moaning. When he slammed the trunk shut, we were in total darkness. I felt so trapped. I'm the one with claustrophobia.

"If this is a car jacking why doesn't he just take the car? What does he want with us?" Melanie wailed.

"Mel, I recognize those glasses. And that voice. That is Roger Craighead."

The engine started and the car was rolling.

"And I'll tell you what he wants with us. The gold. He's onto us. He figured out we withheld that second page of the will because there was something written on it that we didn't want him to see. Confirmation that the legend was true. That there really was a fortune in gold."

"So what is he going to do with us? We don't know where it is?"

The car came to a stop, then turned right. We were at the end of Melanie's driveway and he was turning onto Airlie Road toward the Waterway.

"He doesn't know that. Remember Amy Wood telling us he asked permission to look around her land with a metal detector? For military artifacts, he said. And she also told us that someone was skulking around at night and she thought it was Dewey Carter. It was Roger. Spying on her. Searching for the gold."

"Well, we don't know where it is. What does he want with us?"

"Mel, he doesn't know that. He may think . . . Ouch! Watch your knee."

"Sorry, but I'm cramped. Where are we anyway?"

"I think we're on Airlie Road, driving out toward Eastwood."

"But where is he taking us?"

"My guess? Somewhere secluded. Maybe out on the beach where he thinks we'll be alone and he can question us about the gold. If only there was a way out of here."

"This car has GPS. Cam will call the police. They'll trace the car. They'll find us. Oh, we're stopping."

"We must be at Eastwood. I hear the siren. The bridge is going up."

"At this hour?"

"They open it on request. If they are opening the bridge, he must be waiting. Change of plans. Trying to make a left turn instead of taking the bridge. There must be traffic backed up on Eastwood."

Then I spotted it. "Mel, what is that shiny thing I see? It kind of glows in the dark."

"Oh, cripes, where is my mind? I'm so panicky I can't even think. My salesman showed me that thing. It's an escape latch. Can you reach it? My arm is pinned under me."

"Can you scoot over? I can't lift my head. But if you scoot over I can get my hand up there."

We shifted around, banging knees and elbows. Then my hand was free and I grabbed the latch and pulled it. And miracle of miracles, the trunk popped open.

There was light. And precious air. And I was right. We were at Eastwood just at the drawbridge approach.

We scrambled out of the trunk, holding onto each other, falling onto the pavement, helping each other up. Roger would have heard and felt the trunk open. He'd be after us.

"The bridge!" I yelled. "Run up the ramp."

"But the bridge is opening," Melanie cried.

"It's not open yet. The arm isn't down. We can't go back. Everything is closed up. He'll corner us. Hurry! Hurry!"

We ran up the pedestrian ramp. A railing separated us from the few cars stopped in the car lanes. Beneath us in the water, two tall ships waited to sail through.

"Come on," I called over my shoulder. "There's a guy up there in that glass booth tending the bridge. We'll get help."

Melanie paused to kick off her high heels. I turned back and grabbed her by the hand. "He's coming!" I cried. "There's no time to stop."

The siren was a warning that the bridge was about to open. Then the arm would go down and the bridge would start to lift into two separate sections. I prayed we had time and didn't get trapped.

There were popping sounds as bullets whizzed by us. "He's shooting at us!" Melanie screamed.

Just as we reached the top of the ramp, the bridge's arm began lowering in front of us. "Hurry, we can get under it," I shouted.

We ducked and hustled under the arm just as the noise and vibration sounded under our feet. "It's opening," Melanie screamed.

"Jump! Jump!"

Holding hands we jumped from one side of the bridge to the other. Roger was still after us. Shooting wildly.

We scrambled away from an opening that led straight down into the water. The opening grew larger and the bridge began its upward slant.

But if we could clear the parting bridge, Roger thought he could too. The man in the bright red Santa suit leapt into the air. Then disappeared from sight.

17

"That heavy Santa suit weighed him down," Walt Brice said. "The Coast Guard is searching for his body. It'll surface. But the Waterway current is swift. They think he'll float up somewhere downstream."

On Sunday afternoon, we were gathered in my library. My family and our attorney, Walter Brice. What a night we had suffered through. The EMTs checking us over. The Wrightsville police. The Coast Guard. Even Homeland Security questioned us. In the early morning hours we were released and sent home to try to get some sleep. Hopefully to sleep away the horrors of being shot at on the bridge.

"It's a blessing our darling girls survived their ordeal," Aunt Ruby said. She was holding little Jonnie on her lap. Or was it Peter?

Scarlett's eyes were fairly popping. "Every time I come here to Wilmington you are involved in some life-threatening criminal case. My life on Broadway is tame by comparison."

"I agree," her husband Ray said. "You guys live on the edge here. Wall Street is nothing like Wilmington."

"What other news do you have, Walt?" Cam asked. He was seated on the couch, Melanie in his arms. He had vowed he was never letting her go. Jon and Cam, and our family, had been frantic when they'd come out of the house last night and found us and the car gone. They'd left the babies with Aunt Ruby and jumped into the Escalade to start out Airlie Road in search of us. When they got to Eastwood, they were caught in traffic. A driver had abandoned a car at the intersection. They didn't know the car was Melanie's or that the fleeing driver was Roger Craighead. Then all Hell broke loose with emergency vehicles racing for the bridge.

"What other news do you have about the case?" Ray asked.

Walt settled back in an arm chair and tented his finger-tips, a gesture I had come to recognize as meaning he was about to impart important information. "Regina Redfield has returned. And she is singing like a canary."

"But where was she?" Melanie asked.

"According to Lieutenant Edmunds, she's been at Bald Head Island. Seems she has a listing over there, an unoccupied house for sale, and she was hiding out in it. She walked to the ferry at Southport and took it to the island, then used a golf cart to get to the house."

"What else did he say?" I asked.

"It was a matter of the falling out of thieves," Walt replied. "In this case, the falling out of murderers. Mrs. Redfield and her nephew Roger are behind the killings. She just got sick of her husband's philandering and his ineptitude.

When she found him foundling the babysitter at your flotilla party, Melanie, that was the last straw. She shoved him down the stairs. He was supposed to be controlling Senator Henry, but he couldn't even do that, she complained, not even after they'd provided substantial bribes. She just lost it. Was fed up with the man. She shoved him and he fell on the stairs and broke his neck. But she professes that it was an accident, that she was simply angry, and did not mean for him to die."

"I just know she was the one who tried to shove me in the lagoon at Airlie," Melanie said.

Cam nodded his agreement.

"How did Roger get involved?" Binkie said. "He had a promising career at the university."

"We don't know if she persuaded him or if the conspiracy was his idea," Walt said. "She's blaming him. Their original plan was to get Senator Henry to sponsor a bill that would let them set up a gambling casino at the marina. They thought they'd make a bundle off that. You know, the house always wins.

"When that didn't work out and they realized Senator Henry was going to be a formidable opponent against them, they decided to get rid of him. Only Mrs. Redfield insists it was Roger who laced the coffee with oxycodone. She claims all she did was lure Henry to the house with the promise of sex. She said she thought that when they got him there, she and Roger were just going to discuss the gambling bill, try to persuade Henry to change his mind. She said she would never have participated in murder. That she didn't even know the coffee was laced with a drug until Henry lost consciousness."

"But she didn't call 9-1-1 to save him," I protested. "And Roger Craighead is not here to challenge her version of the story."

"You can be sure the D.A. will be skeptical. They may have enough to charge her with conspiracy to murder. She does admit to being there and to luring Henry to the house. And her hair was found on the bed where he died. Probably they'll bring a charge of manslaughter for Redfield's death. She did admit to shoving him down the stairs. She'll get eight to ten for that, most likely. And much longer if she is convicted of Henry's death. Mrs. Redfield is going to be out of circulation for a long time."

"What a waste," Aunt Ruby said.

"Save your pity, Aunt Ruby. She was out to destroy me," Melanie said.

Walt interjected, "Oh, and one final bit of information. According to Mrs. Redfield, Wren Redfield's oxy supplier was none other than Roger Craighead. Working on campus he had an opportunity to meet drug dealers. They're always hanging around college campuses."

"But why did Roger go after us?" Melanie asked.

"The quest for gold," Walt replied. "When the gambling casino idea fell through, he decided to put his efforts into finding a legendary treasure. And he thought you knew where it was hidden or had a clue as to where it was hidden. I venture to guess, he planned to take you out on a secluded beach and force you into the water if you didn't tell what you knew. He couldn't know that a couple of sailors would call ahead and arrange for the drawbridge to be raised so he couldn't drive to the beach."

"We should have shown you that will right away, Walt," Melanie said. "But I brought it with me today. I'd like you to take a look."

Melanie got up and returned with a large envelope. She slid the contents out and handed the large folded sheets to Walt. He took his time studying the documents. When he was finished, he asked, "Who else knows about this?"

"Just us," I said.

"Just family," Binkie affirmed.

"Ray and I won't breathe a word," Scarlett said.

"You didn't tell Amy Wood, did you, Ashley?" Melanie asked.

"No," I said. "I didn't tell anyone."

"Let's keep it that way. I'm your family lawyer. I can't divulge what you have told me. Attorney-client privilege."

"So you think there might be something to this fortune?" Cam asked.

"I think it deserves checking out."

"My stars," Aunt Ruby exclaimed. "With all the excitement I almost forgot. We've got tickets to the North Carolina Symphony tonight. It's the annual Pops Christmas Concert. I say, let's go. Why let Roger Craighead spoil our holidays any more than he already has."

"Aunt Ruby," Jon interjected. "I'm afraid you can't go. We need you to babysit."

"What!" I exclaimed. "Jon!"

"Wait, hear me out. I think we will also have to share the information about the gold with Amy Wood, as well."

"You're going to have to explain yourself, Jon," Binkie said.

"Jon, what is going on?" I asked.

My husband grinned at all of us. "As you know, I've been working with a computer program that automatically measures the rooms in Amy's house from photos I took, and then produces architectural drawings. Well, I kept getting an error message. I couldn't understand what the problem was. I had to delve deeper into the program.

"And what I discovered is this. The reason I got an error message was because the inside measurements of the rooms do not total the outside dimensions of the house." He grinned mischievously, waiting for us to get it.

"A secret room!" Cam exclaimed.

At six o'clock it was almost dark as we headed down Plantation Road. We had to wait until Amy finished her shift at the medical center to meet us at the house.

Ray and Scarlett stayed at my house to assist Aunt Ruby with the babies. Binkie came with us; we all felt his expertise as a historian might be of assistance in our hunt. And Walt Brice insisted on coming along. As our attorney, he planned to document the find – if there was one – with a video camera.

On the trip down we listened to the car radio anxiously for news. The six o'clock local news on WHQR announced that the body of Roger Craighead, an associate professor of History at UNCW, had been found by the Coast Guard in the waters near Bradley Creek Marina. We also learned that the New Hanover County District Attorney was charging Regina Redfield with the murder of Senator Buddy Henry and with manslaughter for the death of her husband, Wren Redfield.

"She'll be convicted," Walt assured us from the back seat.

Amy met us at her front door. "What is this all about?" she asked after she had been introduced to Cam, Binkie, and Walt. "You sounded so mysterious on the phone."

"Why don't we all sit down and I'll explain, Amy," Jon said. Melanie had brought the will which Amy had never seen before although she remembered her grandfather claiming there was an old will from Samuel Wood. The house and land had been passed down from father to son, but the original will had disappeared. How it got into my father's possession, we would never know, but perhaps as a judge he was researching legal documents when he died.

"Wilmington treasure? Whatever does that mean?" Amy asked as she read the will.

Jon and I took turns explaining about the legend of Cornwallis's gold. Jon told Amy about the error in his computer program that led him to find a discrepancy with the outside and inside measurements of her house. "We'd like your permission to search your house. And your help. Are you aware of any rooms that don't seem to be the size you'd expect them to be?"

Amy got very excited. "I am! The dining room adjoins the parlor yet one wall isn't quite where you'd expect it to be. The room should extend behind the staircase but it doesn't. It's like there is a missing piece to the house."

"Then that's where we'll start," Jon said. "Show us."

Amy led the way into the dining room. "What are we looking for?" she asked.

"Some interruption in the architecture. A cabinet. Something like that."

"What about that corner cupboard?" Amy asked.

I was vibrating with excitement. "It's in the corner where you'd expect the wall to extend further back. We'll have to unload the cabinet, Amy."

"Sure. Put the dishes on the table." Amy opened the glass paned door and we all began removing plates, cups, and saucers and stacked them on the table. Walt started the video camera and recorded us as we worked. "I've shut off the audio," he said, "so feel free to say whatever you like. I think it's wise to document this search in the off chance we do find something valuable."

When the cabinet was empty, Amy asked, "What now? Will there be a catch or a hinge or something?"

"Probably nothing as sophisticated as that," Jon said. "But look, Amy, you can see that the corner cupboard is not truly built in. The framing is not contiguous with the wood trim on the wall. There are seams. We're going to have to see if we can drag it out of the corner."

Jon and Cam took hold of either side of the cupboard and rocked it a bit to see if it would move. It did. Then it was a matter of lugging the heavy piece of furniture away from the corner.

"A door," I cried. Behind the cupboard was a small door in the wall. There was no door knob protruding, just a flat lock.

"It's locked," Jon cried as he tried pushing the door inward.

"I've got some old keys," Amy said excitedly. She left the room and returned with a large key ring that was loaded with keys.

"Let me," Jon said, taking the key ring from her and then one by one trying each in the lock.

"This is a historical moment," Binkie said softly, as if in awe of what we were doing.

"OK, I've got it," Jon cried. "Everyone gather round. You'll all want to see this." The door was stuck and took some pushing. "House has settled," Jon said.

Finally the door opened into a small dark room. "I'll get a flashlight," Amy said, and ran from the room. Returning with the flashlight she handed it to Jon and he shone it into the darkness.

"I want to see too," Melanie cried, aiming the flashlight she had brought in from our car.

"I think there is room for all of us," Jon said. "But let's tread carefully. We don't know what we might find."

We slipped inside as Walt filmed our entry. We crowded into the little room, but there was only one item in it. A barrel in a corner. A very old wooden barrel. And on top of the barrel, some folded pieces of cloth.

Carefully, I lifted the pieces, turning to face the camera, and gently unfolded them. "Colonial uniforms," Binkie exclaimed. "Those are British garments that a British soldier might have worn."

"Didn't the legend say that Samuel Wood exchanged articles of his clothing for those of a prison guard?" I said.

"I remember that," Melanie cried.

With the clothing off the barrel, all that remained was the lid. "Shall I?" Jon asked.

"Please hurry," Melanie said. "The suspense is killing me," and she shone her light at the corner.

Jon grasped the edge of the lid and tugged. It came off. Shining the flashlight inside, he exclaimed, "Oh my god!"

"What? What?"

"It's here. It's the gold."

And we all moved in for a look inside the barrel with Walt filming the contents. Shiny gold coins. Binkie stepped forward. "Allow me." He reached into the barrel and held up a golden coin. "Jon, shine the light on this."

We all crowded around to see. "I've been doing some research since we first read and discussed the will. This is a British guinea, about ninety percent pure gold, minted in Great Britain from gold mined in the Guinea region of West Africa. Thus its name. It bears the image of King George III on one side and a crowned shield on the other."

"What is it worth?" Amy asked.

Binkie grinned in the glow of the flashlight. "One of these? About $3,000."

"And there are how many? A thousand?"

"A thousand easily," Jon said, staring into the barrel.

"Three million dollars!" Cam whooped.

"But won't the government claim the gold?" Amy asked worriedly.

"Or the British government?" I asked.

"They can claim all they want to," Melanie said, "they ain't gettin' it."

"Oh, what I could do with just a fraction of this gold," Amy said. "I could endow the Pediatric Trauma unit at the hospital. I could enlarge the animal rescue farm and hire professionals to come work on it. We could rescue animals from all over the country, like that elephant rescue farm in Tennessee."

"I'd use my share for historic preservation," I said, dreaming too. "I'd buy up historic properties all over the state and have them restored. Save our heritage so it'll be there when my babies grow up. What would you do, Mel?"

Melanie thought for a moment. "Water. The world's children need clean drinking water. I'd build wells all over the world. Cam and I could travel to third-world countries and oversee the projects. Like Bill and Melinda Gates."

"We'll set up a foundation," I said. "Oh, we can do so much good with this fortune."

"Does anyone besides us know about the gold and how it got here? How Samuel Wood found it and brought it here?" Cam wanted to know.

"That is just a legend," I said. "No proof. Only the family knows about the will. No one will tell. Ray and Scarlett won't tell. Aunt Ruby surely won't."

"My lips are sealed," Binkie said.

I went on, "We don't have to tell what we know. And we honestly don't know how it got here. It is found treasure. And I believe found treasure belongs to the finders."

Jon interjected, "Roger Craighead suspected but he is dead."

"I rather doubt he told his aunt Regina. He wouldn't want to share," Binkie said.

"And Walt is covered by privilege."

"Good, because we're going to need a lawyer," Jon said.

Walt barked out a laugh. "You're going to need a team of lawyers."

"That's OK," I said with a smile. "We've got the money to pay a team." I moved to Jon's side and threw my arms around him. "How do you like having a rich heiress for a wife?"

Jon smiled happily. "Our wedding vows said for richer or poorer. No offense, but I kinda like the richer part."

"Me too."